THE SIGN OF THE DEVIL

JOHN PICKERSGILL

To Hannah

from John
x

THE SIGN OF THE DEVIL

JOHN PICKERSGILL

Blackie & Co
Publishers Ltd

A BLACKIE & CO
PUBLISHERS LIMITED PAPERBACK

© Copyright 2003

JOHN PICKERSGILL

The right of JOHN PICKERSGILL to be identified as Author of this work has been asserted in accordance with the Copyright, Designs and Patents Act 1988

All Rights Reserved

No reproduction, copy or transmission of this publication may be made without written permission. No paragraph of this publication may be reproduced, copied or transmitted save with the written permission or in accordance with the provisions of the Copyright Act 1956 (as amended). Any person who does any unauthorised act in relation to this publication may be liable to criminal prosecution and civil claims for damage.

First published in 2003

A CIP catalogue record for this title is available from the British Library

ISBN 1-84470-029-1

Blackie & Co Publishers Ltd
107-111 Fleet Street
LONDON EC4A 2AB

Printed and Bound in Great Britain

Dedicated to my mentor

Peter Lambe

CONTENTS

Chapter One 9

Chapter Two 14

Chapter Three 19

Chapter Four 24

Chapter Five 29

Chapter Six 32

Chapter Seven 34

Chapter Eight 36

Chapter Nine 40

Chapter Ten 43

Chapter Eleven 47

Chapter Twelve 55

Chapter Thirteen 58

Chapter Fourteen 61

Chapter Fifteen 64

Chapter Sixteen 68

Chapter Seventeen 72

Chapter Eighteen 77

Chapter Nineteen 82

Chapter Twenty 85

Chapter Twenty One 91

Chapter Twenty Two 96

Chapter Twenty Three 101

Chapter Twenty Four 104

Chapter Twenty Five 111

Chapter Twenty Six 117

Chapter Twenty Seven 122

Chapter Twenty Eight 126

Chapter Twenty Nine 131

Chapter Thirty 140

Chapter Thirty One 142

Chapter Thirty Two 153

Chapter Thirty Three 161

Chapter Thirty Four 169

Chapter Thirty Five 174

Chapter Thirty Six 176

Chapter Thirty Seven 182

Chapter Thirty Eight 192

Chapter Thirty Nine 194

Chapter One

Shelagh Murray gazed dotingly upon her only son Dermott and with casual abandon, she spoke.

'Your father would have been proud of you son, you would make a grand priest, you have the calling for it.'

'No he wouldn't, he likes the girls too much,' retorted his sister Mary.

'I don't too,' interjected Dermott.

'Yes you do. I have seen the way you look at Rosemary when she gets out of the bath.'

He blushed because that much was true, he did look at Rosemary, but not just at Rosemary, he also looked at his other sisters, too. He wondered if this natural disposition would bar him entry from the Priesthood, but the more he thought about it, the more he reasoned that this should not be a stumbling block, after all, there were other things which troubled him more.

Firstly, there was *the* matter, which was related to his subconscious and his innate ability, to desecrate, those things, which were regarded as sanctimonious. And secondly, he wondered if the devil had captured his mind, because his mother, albeit in a jovial manner, referred to him as Beelzebub whenever misfortune invaded the Murray household.

He had been born as the only boy, into a large Catholic Irish family on 6-6-1966 and there was nothing significant about this, save that his mother had been taught in *her* religious upbringing, that this date was somehow associated with the devil. Being able to quote many passages from the bible she noted, therefore, the book of Revelation did indeed refer to the numbers 666, as the sign of the devil. Whilst she didn't necessarily read too deeply into this, in her innermost heart, she secretly wished that her son had been born into the world on a different date.

Shelagh herself, born in Dublin in 1938, had shared in the beauty for which its females were proverbial: but that beauty had gradually withered beneath the heavy toll of trying to bring up a large family on a very limited budget. Now she was meagre, pale and sometimes sickly-looking. Her once pretty face was lined and wrinkled, brought about by excessive smoking and the constant worry of trying to keep her daughters and son on the right path through life, and also towards spiritual salvation.

She had long lost her Irish accent but hung onto the Irish traditions of having a great regard for everything touching the Catholic faith, and expected the same from her offspring. She insisted that the family prayed together regularly and added an old adage, 'The family that prays together stays together.'

Dermott's sisters felt that this was idiosyncratic trivia, a remnant of a bygone age and they refused to participate in such melodramatic nonsense, but Dermott felt obliged to do so, after all he was the only male in the household.

There were one or two other matters however, which would have not only barred his entry to the church but, which would have seen him excommunicated from it, had the clergy discovered the facts behind the truth. Both these incidents occurred when Dermott was aged fourteen and was an altar boy at his local church. One day, the parish priest had been called back to the rectory urgently. He had inadvertently left the safe door ajar where the consecrated hosts were stored. Dermott's companion peered inside and jokingly said, 'I'm hungry, let's have a bit of bread,' and with that extracted several of the Eucharistic wafers proffering them to Dermott. Stuffing them into his mouth, he blurted out, 'Fancy a glass of wine to wash them down?' and reached over to the cupboard where the blessed altar wine was kept. He took a large swig before offering the bottle to his friend, who did likewise, both of them laughing and giggling in the process. Then panic set in. What if the priest, on his return, could smell the drink on the breath of the two boys? Quick as a flash, Dermott poured some wine on to the sacristy floor so that the room, now smelled, somewhat like a wine cellar. When the priest returned, Dermott instantly owned up to having spilt some wine on the floor whilst filling the wine crucible. He was severely rebuked and told to be far more careful.

'This wine has been consecrated and is about to be turned into the blood of Christ,' declared the priest in a despairing manner. This event had been a close call and both boys had escaped by the skin of their teeth.

Afterwards, however, a feeling of severe guilt and remorse had set in Dermott's mind and he felt he would have to confess this very grave sin, to the priest he had so cleverly concealed his crime from. But when his time came in the confessional box, he disguised the sin as one he had committed in the past, and could not now remember. As he sat in the wooden benches reciting his penance, gloomy thoughts entered his mind. To have drank the wine and partaken of the holy bread, had either been very foolhardy, or very wicked, or both. These were the very rudiments that were used in the transubstantiation and offered to the congregation.

He shuddered. My God, he thought to himself, I must be mad or even worse, 'evil'. He and his companion had desecrated the body and blood of Christ!

There had also been another event of a not dissimilar nature, around Easter time, when everyone including 'Uncle Tom Cobleigh' and all, invaded the church to make their annual confession, in order to reconcile them with God.

At this church, the priest made his entrance to the confessional box via the sacristy and the congregation, from a separate door in the church itself. One evening, the two boys arrived early to prepare the altar before the 'Benediction' service. Dermott turned to his friend with a singular smile on his face.

'I have been a bad boy father, will you hear my confession?'

His friend turned back giggling.

'What me?'

'Yes, you father, now.'

'Don't be mad, I am not the priest.'

'Yes, but you can be,' laughed Dermott handing over the chasuble, the priest's outer garment.

'We will get caught.'

'No we won't, he won't be here for ages yet.'

'I can't do it.'

'Well, I will be the priest and you can be the penitent,' scoffed Dermott, placing the chasuble over his head, and at the same time bursting into fits of uncontrollable laughter, because the garment was about four sizes too big for him, and it trailed along the floor, as he entered into the confessional box.

'Quick, round the other side and let me hear your sins.' His partner in crime, glanced around checking no one was yet in the church, and then, unable to contain his laughter also, stumbled into the box. In fits of amusement, he began.

'Father can you bless me because I have been a naughty boy?'

Dermott assumed the sombre voice of a priest, and deliberately stifled his laughter.

'What have you done my son?'
'Well I thought about this girl at school and started playing with myself.'
'You did what?' interjected the *imitation* priest. Maniacal laughter ensued as the sinner could no longer contain himself.
'I started p-l-a-y-i-n-g with myself.'
Dermott's voice became more rigid as he acted the part out with great diligence.
'Well, my son, this is a very grave matter, very grave indeed,' and with that, he delivered his next words, in the most authentic tone he could muster. 'I will have to refer the matter to the Bishop, and we know what he will do, he will arrange to have it chopped off!' Fits of scornful laughter rent the roof as the two companions ended their shameful game, and Dermott tripped over the priest's garment which was acting more as a floor duster than the holy cloth it was supposed to be.

Several days later, Dermott was once again riddled with remorse over this latest incident and he made an effort to attend mass seven days running as atonement for this blasphemous act. From aged about seven until about 14, his natural innocence had rendered his conscience so delicate, that he was much more affected than his older sisters by the knowledge that he might not be in a state of permanent grace. He worried about it. Sin in his young soul rendered him miserable, often sulky and disobedient, and in this disturbed state of mind, his capacity to do anything properly and his efforts to dispel his unhappiness, often plunged him deeper into offences against God, and into consequent greater misery. His scruples troubled him often.

His mother did not help matters as she would manipulate her family for her own ends and indeed, she was feared and despised by several of her brood, including Dermott. If she didn't get her own way, she would scream and rant until she did. If that particular ploy did not work, she would resort to another Irish trick of breaking down in tears, and at the same time, insisting that no one appreciated her or loved her.

'What have I done that God could give me such an uncaring family?' she could be frequently heard to say, with lips pouting and body language portraying that of a spoilt child. Dermott was easy meat for her because she simply played on his insecurity. She encouraged his belief that he was worthless and in that way, kept an absolute hold over him. She had taught him that the first great virtue of youth was obedience to parents.

'Honour your father and your mother, that you may be long lived upon the land,' she would repeat, until both Dermott and his sisters sick of hearing this, would mimic her behind her back. 'Of what does this honouring consist?' Dermott would question, to which the reply came, 'It consists in obeying, respecting and helping your parents. When you are given a command, you should carry it out promptly, without any show of discontent.'

'Yes mother' he would reply, and he would shrug his shoulders or shake his head instead of answering back.

Although he was insecure, Dermott hid this trait behind his extroverted personality, and he had many attributes.

He was intelligent, of that there was little doubt. The broad deep forehead, the alert blue eyes, the expressive lips, the determined curve of the chin, together with an air that was at once self possessed and modest: all suggested to the experienced eye, that he was an unusually gifted spirit. He also had a warm heart when it suited his purpose and was a good listener and yet there was a sinister side to his nature. He could be spiteful and vengeful as if he were getting back at a world that had dealt him a raw deal. Still, his religious upbringing had ensured that he did not wander too far off the correct path and he developed a warm affection for most of the teachings of the church. 'Perhaps I should become a priest' he often thought, 'it will help me keep on the straight and narrow path and I will be able to live with my conscience that bit easier because I will be offering myself to God.'

Chapter Two

At aged 18, he realised some serious decisions about his future had to be taken. He had taken to the hills for a few days, in order to get away from it all and so that he could do some clear thinking. He turned the corner and began walking into the remote valley, which on a clear day would have revealed a myriad of peaks. But today, the mist was like fog and it was almost down to the bulldozed track as he trudged along into the hinterland. He knew that when he took to the mountains he would be able to think with great clarity and make some positive decisions. He struggled to find the stream in the mist, which was his guide up the hillside. Out came his compass and now he was fumbling with cold fingers to take the correct bearing from the map, which he hoped would lead him to the summit ridge. At around 2000ft, however, a golden splendour beheld him. He plunged out of the mist and into a new world. Blue skies everywhere and not a wisp of cloud. Glaciated peaks abounded and the air was crystal clear, so that every minor hill and bump stood out on the horizon like a mini 'Matterhorn' waiting to be conquered.

This was a cloud inversion on a grand scale and the well-trodden valleys were completely obliterated, whilst the sun shone down through an azure sky. This was why he had come and he would be able to get his thoughts in perspective as the day unfolded.
'Now, for the summit ridge,' he muttered to himself. He liked a challenge, particularly a challenge he could surmount on his own, without the interference of his 'family' or more particularly, his mother, who was always telling him what he should do with his life. If he joined the church, he would be able to do as he pleased and make all his own decisions without having to consult a second party.
He got into some real difficulty on rocks below the summit because the snow and ice had glazed them over and it took one or two hair-raising moments and a bucket full of sweat to negotiate a route to the top. The panorama was the finest he had ever seen. Peak after peak silhouetted in sharp contrast against a perfect winter sky, looking exactly like a scene from an alpine range. He reached the summit trig point, took out his camera and then reached for his

hot flask of tea. He looked all around and began to savour the view, his thoughts well away from the troubled world he had left behind. He could 'hear' and 'feel' the silence, a truly wonderful experience and once more, the demons evaporated from his mind. He enjoyed the stunning views from the summit for over half an hour and then thought about setting off back down to the valley. He scraped his ice axe on the frozen rocks and as he did so, looked at the sharp pointed spike and shuddered involuntary as thoughts from the past invaded his mind. He suddenly remembered the day, when at only eight years of age, he had accidentally pushed his sister Louise, who then tumbled, from a tree and impaled herself on the spikes of a railing. She had been lucky to survive the incident and even today, she still carried a horrible scar across her stomach where the spikes had penetrated. Yes, Beelzebub was his name all right because all the disasters surrounding the Murrays were in some small or large way connected to his self.

'If I joined the church,' he thought, 'I could shake off this stigma and dispel this myth once and for all.' He set off following the footprints he had made on his ascent of the mountain thinking about what was required of him if he was to enter the church.

Everyone who comes to believe in the Christ is obliged to enter into the deepest and fullest relationship with him. To know God, but to decide to keep him at arm's length, as an acquaintance, would be absurd. The bond with Christ was mystical, invisible, but through the Church, there existed a visible bond. There were the sacred scriptures and an entire sacramental system, which was a means of making one holy and a wealth of disposable resources for discovering the truth of God in Christ.

'The truth of God in Christ'. He wasn't sure about that one. One of the standard criticisms of faith was that it was looked upon as a form of special pleading, and therefore, as dishonest. How, he asked himself, was it possible to believe in something, which could not be proved or understood?

Because of his failings and his troubled conscience, he wasn't sure if he had found Christ for sure but he believed the Catholic account of the gospel was true as no other was true and that surely, was enough to gain entry to Holy Orders. Within the church was the full ministry, priest, bishop, Archbishop, just how high could he rise?

He arrived back at the lay-by and noticed another car parked next to his own which had not been there in the morning. He caught a glimpse of someone, half in and half out of this car, trying to remove their walking boots. He looked a little closer at the same time trying not to appear as if he was staring. He spied a stunning young woman with hair as black as jet and it reminded him of his sister Mary. She was wearing a blue cagoule and with her slender fingers, she was tugging at the muddy bootlaces. He could see that she had a well-turned leg and he was distracted by her overall appearance. He struggled for something to say but she spoke first.

'It's been a grand day,' she said.

'Yes, these days are few and far between. I came to find some peace and quiet and I was not disappointed.'

'Yes, me too. I was in a world of my own up on the ridge.' He was beginning to enjoy the few words of exchange, as women of this calibre were not prone to taking to the hillsides alone.

He was about to continue but she interjected.

'Well, I have to be going, I have a long drive, nice speaking with you.'

'Yes, you too,' and in a moment, she started her car and drove off down the muddy track.

For some reason, he felt a heavy heart and he thought to himself that this young lady would have made a very suitable partner. Then, he then questioned this reasoning, but you don't even know her. Then, thoughts of Teresa came into his mind.

Teresa was a cousin from Ireland with whom he had formed a warm adolescent relationship in the summer months when she had come to stay with the family. It had been a hot day, the sun red and flaming, its scorching rays burning into the hillside, and he had accidentally brushed against her. It had only been a fleeting moment, but he had smelt her fragrance, which had immediately aroused his senses. She had smiled back at him with warm searching looks that almost melted his heart. Despite their tender age, their natural disposition revealed itself.

On another occasion, they had been strolling back to the house hand in hand when his mother had spied them.

'What in God's name are you doing? Get into that house at once and leave Teresa alone.'

'I'm not doing anything,' he replied.

'To bed and say your prayers and ask forgiveness for holding Teresa's hand too closely.'

He was confused by severity of her tone, but reflected on the pleasure his senses had beheld hand in hand with Teresa. Now, as usual, he was troubled by his conscience. He felt sure he had committed a sin and prayed earnestly for forgiveness. This triggered the usual dark thought in his mind.

'The devil has captured my mind otherwise I wouldn't feel so guilty!'

Dermott and his three sisters knew little about Teresa except that she was the daughter of Josie, Shelagh's younger sister. They had sometimes asked about Teresa's father but had been severely rebuked by Shelagh by this enquiry.

'Don't pester me now, I am busy, ask me later.' But no one ever dared to. The tone of her voice was sufficient to deter the boldest of characters.

Teresa was lively and gay and prone to being coquettish, and although she ruled by a look, a word or a gesture, she respected Dermott for his openness of heart and the proud boldness of his character.

It was the day before Teresa was due to go back to Ireland. They fell behind the rest of the picnic party. Teresa was trying to fix her shoelace. Thick drops of rain began to tumble from the sky.

'I'm cold.' Teresa said instinctively. He linked his arm between hers and pulled her more closely.

He could scarcely contain himself and he turned and looked into her young and beautiful face, her eyes as velvety as the gazelle's.

Then they were kissing. Not exactly a proper kiss, but he had allowed his lips to linger just that fraction longer than was expected. And he was sure he had felt the warmth of her spontaneity. He kissed her a second time and this time she yielded to his embrace, both of them slightly confused as to what was happening. He was becoming aroused. He suddenly stopped.

'My God!' he yelled 'we will be in big trouble for this.'

'In trouble with whom?' she whispered.

'Shelagh, God, everyone.'

'Don't be silly, no one knows, there is not a soul about.' He tried to recoil but she pulled him closer. His hands began to explore parts of her body and now he fell clumsily on top of her in a passionate embrace.

'Gently,' she whispered' Gently, Dermott, your hands are so strong.'

Five minutes elapsed. Five minutes went by and now they had grown together like two trees whose roots are mingled, whose branches intertwine, and whose perfume rise together to the skies, and then their passion spent, they lay together both exhausted and confused at the same time.

Since that day, flashbacks had intruded his mind on a regular basis. He thought fondly, no passionately, about the act he had committed with his beloved Teresa. But almost simultaneously, another thought tormented him. His was most definitely in league with the devil! He had been a willing party to an act, not an adult act, but one that was regarded as extremely sinful out of wedlock. He blamed himself of course; his righteousness would not let any condemnation fall on his beloved Teresa. He often thought of her. She had become his soul partner and no other person had yet discovered *their* secret. Secretly they had exchanged addresses and he had written to her on at least two occasions. But he had not received a reply. What was the problem? The postman had not called at his door and he had secretly looked in his mother's diary to try to find a telephone number, any number, which would make reference to Teresa. But it was to no avail, nothing could he find. Did she not feel for him in that special way?

He was suffering. Tortured. Mental torture brought about by his own guilt. A letter from her would have helped ease the pain, ease the guilt, which was now burrowing like a termite in the recesses of his mind. If she had been around, if she had replied to his letter, he would have had second thoughts about joining the priesthood. He missed her. Didn't he? No, this was just his basic instinct rising to the surface. Priest or no priest, these lustful tendencies were not going to disappear. Surely, all the clergy had such thoughts. It was no reason to shy away from a vocation and his mother would be ever so proud of him. And even with this positive thought, he shuddered in spite of himself.

Chapter Three

He made his announcement on 1st November 'All Saints' Day', an important day in the calendar of the church. His mother was overjoyed. 'Dermott, I always knew why God put you on this earth. It was to become a priest and serve the Lord.'

'You must be mad,' interjected Mary.

'They will throw you out, you haven't got a vocation. You will be cooped up with all those men and you will want to be out with the girls!'

'I am not interested in the girls.'

'Who are you trying to kid?'

'You are interested in Teresa, admit it.' His cheeks coloured up.

'I am not bothered about the girls and I don't even know where Teresa is.'

'She is in Dublin.' Shelagh casually remarked. Dermott pricked up his ears. This was the first time his mother had yielded any information about Teresa.

'Where in Dublin?' he asked.

Shelagh suddenly realised she had overshot the mark, and she added quickly.

'Dermott, Dublin is a big city, I can't remember exactly without looking it up. I will write and tell her the good news.'

'Why don't I write to her myself,' he said trying to appear as nonchalant as possible.

Shelagh hesitated as if weighing up something in her mind.

'No, I will write to her, Dermott. It will be the proudest letter I will ever have to write.'

Dermott felt a wave of emotion pass over him and felt his heart dilate and throb, but he was not about to get an opportunity to mail his *love* and he so desperately wanted to hear from her.

Evening shadows appeared and rain was hammering on the windows outside. The Murray household was settling down for slumber, but sleep would not visit Dermott's eyelids, on this cold and dark November evening. His mind was racing and yet he could hear someone moving about downstairs. He slipped noiselessly out of bed and by peering over the banister rail, he could make out the shadowy form of Shelagh moving in and out of the alcove under the stairs. He could hear the sound of what appeared like papers, being shuffled around and then Shelagh sat at the table to scribble a few notes down and at the same time, yawned as if yearning for her bed. Dermott returned quietly to his room in avoidance of being discovered as the *voyeur*. It was not until 2.30am that his mind rested, although somewhat fitfully.

Morning arrived and he was physically weary but mentally alert, for the scene he had witnessed the previous evening had aroused his suspicion. Dermott was interested in visiting the old battered briefcase under the stairs. Not exactly a briefcase, more like a leather holdall with a lock and key.

He had access to this holdall, but not to the key. He would bide his time. Thursday evening would be a good time. Usually, Dermott was left alone for several hours whilst the girls and their mother were out at the shops. He waited with some impatience until they had driven away. Moving toward the recess under the stairs, he was immediately consumed with guilt.

'Satan has taken hold of my senses again,' he murmured to himself.

Why would his mother wish to keep papers hidden away under the stairs? The holdall had been there for years and it had never crossed his mind anything interesting would be contained therein.

It was as he expected locked. He sought to open it; it was impossible, the lock remained firm. This faithful guardian was unwilling to surrender its trust.

He managed to procure a screwdriver and inserted the sharp end into the lock. The holding mechanism now gave way and the jaws of the lock opened. Panic now ensued, however, because the lock was scratched and damaged, a sure sign of his intrusion, but he dispelled this thought as quickly as it had arisen. He upturned the leather holdall and a pile of papers, held tightly with a rubber band and paper clip, fell into a heap to the floor. The first item to catch his eye was a crumpled white envelope, ink stained as if it had been left out in the rain. He picked it up and began to examine this envelope. Then he started as if seized by vertigo and stood motionless with amazement. It was addressed to him! In his excitement, he tore at the envelope and the letter fell to the floor at the same time leaving the envelope in two pieces. He began to scrutinise the contents. Had a thunderbolt fallen into the room, he could not have been more stupefied. It was from Teresa, professing her innermost feelings, towards Dermott, and asking why had he not written back to her. He rummaged through the assortment of papers and found yet another letter addressed to him. The date on the first envelope preceded the other by two months or so. He became confused and angry at the same time. Why would have his mother hidden these away from him? They belonged to him, no one else. Not only had she intruded in his life again, she had now desecrated these most private exchanges. He read and re-read both letters. My God, he thought, Shelagh has read both these, she must have surmised something had happened between these young and tender hearts. He was now thinking of how to replace the documents in their receptacle without it looking as if the contents had been disturbed, when he spied another bundle of papers held tightly together with a large metal clip. He removed the retaining clip and realised that the top document was a birth certificate. It was his own certificate. Lying underneath this document were those belonging to his sisters – all three of them and his mind subconsciously counted them by name; Mary, Rosemary, and Louise.

At first, he thought he had made a mistake and he re-counted them, one, two, three, four, including his own. But there appeared to be five and this time he physically laid them down on the floor.
'One, two, three, four, five,' he said out loud. The fifth one, he thought, must belong to his mother. He began to examine the documents individually.
'Mary, Rosemary, Louise, and Dermott,' he said to himself.
He examined them all noting all similarities. He carefully noted that both his mother's and father's name, were mentioned on all the four documents. But Dermott had never known his father. Shelagh and Desmond Murray had been unable to reconcile their differences. Desmond drank himself into a state of insensibility with frequent regularity leaving Shelagh black and blue in the process. Shelagh had managed to blot out any memories she held for Desmond quite successfully. And so, too, had Dermott's sisters. Their father's name was *never* mentioned even in vane.
His mind began to wander, thinking of the upbringing he had had, without his male father figure, and so many thoughts invaded his mind, he almost forgot the task he had embarked upon. He picked

up the fifth certificate and looked at the bold ink, which stared back at him. His eyes darted from top to bottom and he became spellbound as he read from the document.

Where Born - **3 Poplar Terrace, Dublin**

When Born - **30th August 1968**

Name (if any) - **Teresa**

Sex - **Girl**

Name, surname and maiden surname of Mother :

Shelagh Murray *formerly* **Hannon**

Occupation of Father - **……………………..**

Signature, description and residence of informant:

Shelagh Murray, 3 Poplar Terrace, Dublin

When registered – 14th September 1968

Signature of Registrar – J Moran

There had to be some mistake – some error!

He carefully examined the certificate in great detail and was immediately seized by an uncontrollable fit of trembling. Were he and his sisters closely related to Teresa?

Now he compared the details from his own certificate with that of the fifth one. The one containing details appertaining to Teresa was stamped with GRO Dublin ensignia, whilst his own bore the stamp of St Catherine's House, London. This was slightly confusing for him.

Whatever the relationship was between them both, he could not get away from one overriding fact. He had defiled her body! For a minute or two, he hadn't sufficient clarity of mind to take in what he was reading. His knees felt weak and a misty vapour floated over his eyes as his mind now registered the details on the certificate and he was unable to believe the evidence of his senses. He looked once, and then twice at the details on the parchment. Then, thoughts of imaginary demons and lost souls calling out to him from the dungeon of hellfire overtook his mind. Not for the first time, but this time he could not dispel the train of gloomy spectres, which were beginning to entangle him in a quagmire, and lead him to the door of the abyss. He was now truly convinced that he was an agent of the Devil, and he thought to himself, 'If ever I needed a reason to join the priesthood, then I have one now.' And with that, he re-inforced the vow he had so gingerly announced several hours earlier.

He now had to find a means of restoring lucidity and clearness of mind, for he was truly in a dismal state. For the first half-hour, he felt sure there was some mistake, but as he began to examine his mother's behaviour in his mind, then the plot slowly revealed itself. She had always been guarded if not secretive about everything involving Teresa. One could go so far as to say she was being protective. If what he had read was true (and it had to be) then here then was the explanation for Shelagh's irrational behaviour. But he couldn't fathom the unfathomable and the whole scenario was confusing to say the least. He now possessed some startling information, but just what was he to do with it? He was about to train for the priesthood and he would eventually become a keeper of secrets. The keeper of secrets divulged only in the confessional. He would become accustomed to locking away information such as this from a whole host of penitents, namely the parishioners. 'Yes,' he thought 'I am going to be the guardian of secrets, that is one of the attributes for my vocation.' And with that, he locked the information away until fate determined when it should be revealed to the world again.

Chapter Four

The early years at the seminary passed quickly and without significance and thoughts of hellfire evaporated as he settled into the daily routine of early rising, prayers followed by mass and then the studies for his vocation. When in reflective mood, however, he would ponder for hours and hours, particularly when alone in his study.

Yes, he was somehow related to Teresa of that there could be no question. But now his thoughts were turning obsessive, and he vowed to uncover the real facts as soon as he received his ordination. He addressed his mother during one of her regular visits.

'Have you heard from Teresa lately?' He hoped his surprise enquiry would catch her off guard and that he would elicit some fragment of information. But as usual she was calm and reticent and yielded nothing new.

'Yes, she sends her regards and is so proud about your decision.'

He wasn't comfortable with this last remark because he still hoped somewhere secretly in his heart that she would never forget the special moments they had shared on that rainy afternoon.

However, all thoughts of looking into this matter had for now, taken a back seat. The second year of his studies came and went.

One Sunday evening, he was alone in the church reciting some prayers. January winds were howling outside and the beams of the roof were being battered heavily, creating a feeling of being entombed in a crypt, almost supernatural.

He rose from the kneeler and walked slowly across the church towards the door of the connecting passage, the passage that connected the church to the main part of the building. As he walked, his heels made a clicking sound, which echoed off the church walls, sounding like a pair of castanets being played at a staccato rhythm. He was about to open the side door when he thought he heard something stir at the back of the church. It sounded like a wooden kneeler being scraped on the surface of the church floor. He looked round but could neither see nor hear anyone. Must have been mistaken he thought, but he had the distinct feeling that a pair of secret eyes had been watching him. He got halfway down the passage when he heard the door behind him. He turned round.

'Brother Dermott, I was hoping to catch you.'

'Oh, it's you Michael, you gave me a stir, what can I do for you?'

'Message from Brother Sean, says he and a few others are going on a walk down the abandoned railway track tomorrow. Although it won't be as grand as your mountains, he says you are most welcome. Start is about 3.30pm. Have to rush, not said my novena yet.'

'Strange,' thought Dermott, 'I have never been asked to attend before.' It would not be the same as scrambling up a mountain, but perhaps he would give it a go.

A small group of five was setting off slowly across the fields leading in the direction of the flooded quarry when Dermott, out of breath, rolled up, rucksack in hand.

'Dermott, so pleased you decided to join us, that rounds the numbers up. Let's get going, now we are sure to have a grand day.' It was Sean who spoke and the party set off in high spirits. About halfway down the old railway cutting, Dermott began to notice something was not quite right. The party had somehow become strung out in pairs, which now left Dermott and Sean walking together.

'Hadn't we better wait for the others, I can't even see Michael and Patrick,' said Dermott nervously.

'Let's walk on, us boys together,' returned Sean. Dermott was becoming nervous but was not sure why.

'I'll bet you can be a bit of a lad when you want to be, eh,' Sean continued.

'I am not sure what you mean,' replied Dermott.

'Well, I bet you sometimes fancy a night out with the boys, to give you a break from the studies.'

'Yes, of course, but I chose to give myself to God.'

'Oh yes, but you can't be with God 24 hours a day, that is why we set up the boys' club, to help us enjoy our private time.' Dermott was now very uncomfortable. He didn't like the way the conversation was going. Sean's words were making him feel uneasy.

'Boys' club, what boys' club?' asked Dermott.

'Well, Michael and Patrick, Peter and Francis, you and I.'

Beads of sweat trickled down Dermott's back.

'What's the purpose of this club?'

'To help us gain release from the everyday stresses, of you know, of being cooped up in the seminary.'

'Hadn't we better find the others?'

'No, don't worry, they will be ages yet, just relax. Let's continue, there is a lovely spot just up ahead.' 'My God' thought Dermott, 'I am in a mess here. I am caught up in a gay club. How do I get out of this?' Looking up, he could make out the outline of a rusty old fence, surrounding the perimeter of the quarry and automatically, he headed towards it. He reached it panting, almost out of breath and endeavoured to gather his thoughts before Sean caught him up. He was gazing down on the panorama below when he suddenly felt Sean pat him on the back.

'My God, you are a fit man Dermott,' and with that comment, he moved closer to his friend resting his hand on Dermott's two, outstretched fingers.

'Sean, you are making me feel uncomfortable.'

'Don't be so nervous, just a little pleasure, my young friend.'

'I really should get back, I have a thesis to finish.'

'Well, you are not finished here yet are you?'

'Yes, I am and I am returning now, and if you don't leave me alone I will report this to father guardian.'

'Will you indeed, well that won't do you any good either, you little weed,' and with that comment, Sean released his grip from Dermott, who immediately set off towards the direction of the college.

He had joined the seminary in order to give himself to God and now he was confused.

He really needed to discuss this topic with someone, to somehow vent his feelings on the matter. He was studying now in an environment where trust, confidentiality and the sharing of the problems was an everyday occurrence. Why not share this problem and then hopefully, the burden would be lessened. He hastily arranged an appointment with the rector to discuss his predicament.

Thursday morning arrived as Dermott entered the rector's brilliantly lit room where he found the head pacing up and down. With hardly a word spoken, but with a sharp eye, the rector waved Dermott to an arm-chair.

'What can I do for you, brother Dermott?'

'Well, it is a delicate matter and I am not sure how to start.'

The rector's face fell immediately.

'Father guardian, I joined this college in order to give myself to God and in doing so, I had to give up the pleasures of the world and dedicate myself to a life of celibacy.'

'Yes my son, is that now a problem to you?'

'Well no, but now I feel obliged to let you know that there exists an unhealthy element in certain parts of the college which must be looked into.'

'Dear me!' replied the rector gravely. 'This is very serious, indeed, I am sorry to hear you say that. What exactly is the nature of this unhealthy element that you so readily refer to?'

'Well father, it is a little awkward, as I don't want to incriminate my fellow colleagues. But there are one or two, how can I put this, abnormal characters, about the college. You know, odd.'

'Odd, did you say odd? In what way are they odd?'

'Well father, their disposition is not the same as most of the human race. To put it bluntly, I was approached.'

There was a pregnant pause and the rector now spoke with the voice of a senior with rigid inflexibility of neck and shoulders and his speech became laboured.

'Brother Dermott, what exactly are you trying to say?' Dermott's voice became strangled as he blurted the words out.

'That there is a gay element in the college.' The rector rolled his eyes to the ceiling and then allowed his gaze to fall upon the unfortunate novice before him.

'Dermott my son, would you care to enlighten me further. Just who is involved in this element?'

'Father, I don't wish to name names, as we are all here to work in harmony under God's roof, but you could start with the rambling club. I would rather not go into further detail.'

'Ah, yes, the rambling club,' and his voice tapered off as if he had been interrupted by some overpowering thought.

'Leave it in my hands, brother Dermott.' The young novice made a motion to leave when the guardian continued. 'Oh Dermott, the parish of St Ambrose have asked if we could send someone to talk at a parishioners' evening 3rd Wednesday of next month. The subject will be Morals and the Family in today's society. I thought, perhaps, you could oblige.'

'Well yes, father, if you feel I am up to it.'

'Dermott, with your academic background and personality, we have the ideal candidate. I will notify the parish this very day.' Dermott returned to his room with renewed vigour. Firstly, he was pleased that he had unloaded his burden to the rector and secondly, he had been asked to give a talk to one of the local discussion groups. A feather in his cap for one so young and not yet ordained.

Chapter Five

He was always very thorough in every task he embarked upon and he prepared for this talk with great diligence. Researching writing and then re-writing his speech with great pride. It had come to his notice that these discussion groups were usually advertised in the local press and also in the Catholic press, and afterwards reviewed at great length by the reporters involved. For a moment, he let himself indulge in the vanity of 'seeing his name in print'. He imagined the headline banner 'Brother Dermott delivers *the definitive* argument for 'Morals and the Family in today's society'. Then he restrained himself for his lack of humility. 'That is the devil speaking,' he told himself. He had often made speeches before to his fellow novices with great acclaim, but now this would be for real. Night after night, he practised his speech until his delivery was word perfect and then he prepared answers to the difficult questions he expected to receive. There were three days to go before his talents were to be released to the world and he scoured the local press to see if this talk had been advertised. He could find nothing.

He awoke on the morning of this important day to a black and tempestuous sky and which, for some strange reason, conjured up thoughts of the serpent (the Devil). 'Why am I seized with such gloomy thoughts?' and he forced himself to think positively. The day wore on and suddenly the sky seemed, to him, to become still darker and denser, and compact clouds became lower and lower on the horizon. Suddenly, his study door flung open and in walked the portly figure of the guardian.
'Father guardian, good morning.' But father guardian looked pale and could hardly speak.
'Father, what is the matter?' Dermott continued. But instead of replying the priest held out the paper that he had been clutching tightly. It looked like a newspaper cutting upon which Dermott now cast his gaze. Had a thunderbolt fallen into the room, Dermott could not have been more stupefied. He sank into his seat, and hastily looked once more at the fatal headline with an expression of terror on his face.

It read 'TRAINEE PRIEST ACCUSED OF INDECENT ASSUALT ON FELLOW NOVICE.' But what was more singular was the fact that Dermott's name was written underneath the headline banner and the article quite definitely pointed to *him* as the accused! Dermott, who had minutes earlier been in high spirits, now began to feel a tenfold alarm. The rector now spoke, and his white lips and clenched teeth filled Dermott with apprehension.

'Dermott, the police are in my office waiting to question you about this very grave matter.'

'Father, what is this all about? This must be some huge mistake.'

'Let's go into my office.'

'By all means, I want this to be rectified.' They entered the rector's office, the priest entering first.

A tall thin man with a surly demeanour sat puffing on a cigarette.

'This is brother Dermott Murray.'

The man made no effort to get out of the chair. His body language suggested he had formed a dislike for Dermott before the questioning began. He cautioned Dermott in the usual manner and began asking questions.

'Now,' said the detective, 'answer me frankly, not as a prisoner to a judge, but as one man to another who takes an interest in him, what truth is there in the accusation levelled at you?'

'None at all, I know nothing about these lies.' The policeman threw a letter disdainfully across the desk.

'This letter, to the father here, accuses you of making lewd suggestions and advances and then indecently assaulting one of your fellow colleagues.'

'I know nothing about this, in fact, it was I who reported the opposite to father rector, he will vouch for that, won't you father?'

'Dermott, I think it is time to call in the witnesses and you own up to the matter.'

Dermott became seized like a man with frenzy and now made little resistance. He was now like a man in a dream. He saw the policeman and the rector sat on either side, he answered in monosyllables, he perceived that about ten minutes had elapsed, but all this as mechanically as through a mist, nothing distinctly. They halted for a half-minute, during which he strove to collect his thoughts, but he still could not focus his mind. It was then that the detective motioned to the priest with a nod of the head and Sean,

Patrick and Michael stumbled into the room, with faces composed as if they were gazing upon someone with a contagious disease. Dermott gazed upon them with both, a look of anger and incredibility.

'Now,' said the detective. 'Brother Sean, here, says that you indecently assaulted him up near the old quarry I ask you again is this true?'

'I have told father guardian what happened, he can verify the truth.'

'Dermott, Patrick and Michael were witness to the incident and are willing to substantiate Sean's version of events. Is that not true Patrick?' Instead of speaking, Patrick merely nodded in agreement. Each word fell like a dagger on Dermott and deprived him of a portion of his energy and he fell back on a chair, overwhelmed by wretchedness and despair. He did not reply. He merely looked at his accusers, particularly the rector, with a look, which would strike fear into Satan himself. He then raised his eyes towards the ceiling, hoping the roof would open and reveal first Heaven and then the judge named God. A few moments later, he was led away by the policeman and his colleagues, to start the next stage of his life still cooped up away from the everyday world, but this time it was not of his own choice.

Chapter Six

Dermott's counsel spoke.
'Dermott, it is not looking too clever. The rector swears blind that Sean, Patrick and Michael would never make up such a story, and both he and the Archbishop want to send you for therapy to a special clinic.'
'But I am innocent.'
'I realise that but we need to agree to anything at this moment in time which will help your cause.'
'I expected the church to support me, not treat me as some sort of odd ball.'
'Just go along with it for now, we need as many factors on our side as possible.'
The psychoanalyst was a fat faced man with pink cheeks and a cold eye; he looked at Dermott with his professional gaze without letting any sort of feeling show.
The questioning began in a slow fashion and Dermott answered with a cold indifference. About half way through the session, the questions changed from those of a general nature to something far more personal.
'So, what you are saying then, is that you have never directed your thoughts to the male species even as a schoolboy?' This was the questioner to Dermott.
Dermott tired, frustrated and angry, thought hard for something to say. And then it came to him like the rainbow after the storm. He had an answer, an answer that would put an end to all this bureaucratic nonsense. This was just a way for the church to show to the world that they were dealing with this embarrassing matter. The whole event was cosmetic.
'Listen, if it will help matters, let me tell you about my cousin.'
'Ah yes, your cousin,' replied the pink cheeked man with a singular smile, as if he had just uncorked the most expensive vintage wine money could buy.
'How old is this cousin? Is this someone you look up to?'
'Listen, my cousin is younger than I and a while back now, five years ago to be precise, we had some sort of relationship.'

The psychoanalyst moved his position as if in anticipation of some revelation.

'Was this relationship sexual?'

'Yes it was, just a brief encounter and we have had no contact since.'

'Tell me, do you still have desires for this cousin?'

Dermott paused before he spoke.

'Well yes, but I am soon to take a vow of chastity and celibacy and I cannot turn back from that.'

'Dermott, are you sure you haven't transferred your desire from your cousin to brother Sean?'

'Listen, you old fool, I thought you would realise my cousin is a young woman. I have normal desires, I couldn't have possibly have interfered with Sean.'

The shrink who had been sitting smugly for the last few minutes, now looked uncomfortably placed in his chair. There was a brief silence and then he spoke.

'I think we will have to terminate this interview.' And with that, Dermott was sent back on remand until the outcome of this analysis.

Three days later, the psychoanalyst entered the Archbishop's room and together with the rector, they began to talk. It was the Archbishop who spoke first.

'What are your conclusions then, do you think he is guilty?'

'He referred to a relationship with his cousin, someone named Teresa.'

'It is a difficult one to call but I think he is bisexual.'

'Is that abnormal?' interrupted the Archbishop.

'Well, I guess not so unusual, but he did have some form of actual, sexual contact at such a young age,' and the psychoanalyst's voice trailed off in an unfinished sentence as if he was musing something over in his mind. The conversation continued in a desultory fashion until it appeared that they had all reached the same agreement, Dermott must face up to the consequences of his supposed actions. At least one of the three came away with some inner satisfaction. This incident had attracted bad publicity for the church and the Archbishop believed that the church had to be *seen* to be doing the right thing. Whether the church was doing the *correct* thing was irrelevant.

Chapter Seven

The prosecuting counsel presiding at Dermott's case was a QC named Bradman and all the barristers were frightened of him. He had an evil reputation of being over zealous with his sentencing, particularly in sex cases. And he had an infamous dislike of homosexuals. He stood for the vindication of society and he represented the scales of justice. He would do everything he could to ensure they came down on the right side for him. He stared at Dermott as if he were saying.

'My job is to take all the disgusting evidence against you and make you look so repulsive, that the jury will wish to see you banished from community for a very long time. And what is more, the jury are all proud, of being jurymen and they loathe queers like you who joined the priesthood in order to hide your revolting practices behind a veil. Well let me tell you, you may not see them but there are claws in my heart which are going to rip you to pieces, because I never let my prey escape. Especially little poofs like you.'

Ten o' clock and the trial commenced. The prosecuting lawyer was experienced and going to use all his intelligence to convince the jury that in the first instance Dermott was guilty and secondly, only a custodial sentence was the correct outcome. There was no proof, only the evidence offered by Dermott's three accusers.

Half way through the second session, things were looking black for Dermott.

'You say the witnesses are lying. Why should they wish to lie?'

'I have been accused falsely for not having joined in the disgusting games which these people play.'

'Games, what games are these?'

'The games they play when they go walking up near the old quarry, only the walking is just a camouflage.'

'If you thought they were playing strange games, why did you join them?'

'I didn't know about these games and I reported the incident to father guardian a few days afterwards.'

'Yes and father guardian has told us he can only vouch for the good characters of the three accusers.'

'Yes, I realise that but I don't understand why father guardian supports them, I have told you the truth.'

'So now you are saying that father guardian is a liar?'

'Well, I am certainly not.'

'Well, if you are not, then father guardian is. And may I remind you that in the opinion of the psychoanalyst you have bisexual tendencies!'

A hush of eager anticipation fell over the courtroom and then the prosecuting lawyer spoke again.

'No further questions your honour.' By three in the afternoon the following day, the game of chess was over. It was checkmate for Dermott and his counsel.

'Jury, have you reached your verdict?'

'Yes, your honour.'

'And is that verdict unanimous?'

'It is, your honour.'

'How do you find the accused?'

'Guilty, your honour.'

In the person of Bradman, the prosecuting lawyer society wiped out a young innocent man in the space of about 15 seconds.

'The accused will stand.' Dermott rose to his feet, tears in his eyes and anger in his heart. Most of jury seemed to be looking at the floor or the judge, only one or two stared at Dermott.

'Accused, I have listened to the facts very carefully and men, such as yourself, are a danger to society, especially in a seminary surrounded by other males. The jury's verdict was unanimous but as you have no previous convictions of this nature I am taking a lenient view. You are sentenced to two years in prison, a psychiatric prison, in order to help you adjust to society. Have you anything to say?'

Dermott griped the bar of the dock a little harder.

'Yes, I have. This is a set up by the rector and his cohorts and Satan will have his just reward. The four of them will rot in hell, mark my words.'

Pandemonium broke loose and then the judge yelled out.

'Quiet in my court, take him down.'

Chapter Eight

Tears trickled down Dermott's face, as he was lead down into the bowels of the building. He was glad that his mother and sisters had stayed away from these awful proceedings. He paced up and down his cell, suddenly his breath stopped; I am innocent. Yes, but who was he innocent for? He tried telling himself others must have suffered more but did not gain comfort from this. He was angry with God now. Why had he been forsaken in his hour of need? He suddenly remembered the words he had shouted at the judge, his reference to Satan and then he remembered his birth date once more and a cold shudder passed over his brow.

Dermott passed through all the degrees of misfortune that innocent prisoners left alone in their cell suffer. He commenced with pride a natural consequence of hope, and a consciousness of innocence; then he began to doubt is own innocence, and then falling into the opposite extreme, he supplicated Heaven and the God who had treated him so badly. If he was a servant of the Devil, albeit through the affinity of his birth date, then perhaps this was a punishment from the demon king for offering his life to Jesus. My God, he was becoming confused. He told himself to snap out of it. He entreated to be allowed to walk about freely but mixing with other prisoners for the time being at least, was only allowed at meal and exercise times. He spoke for the sake of hearing his own voice but the sound of his voice terrified him. Before he had been arrested, his mind had revolted at the idea of those assemblages of prisoners, composed of thieves, vagabonds and murderers. Now he occasionally wished to be amongst them in order to see some other face and talk, talk about his innocence to some other human being. Then he thought this would be too comical, as no one would believe him. The prison warders were rude and hardened by the constant sight of so much suffering and Dermott's warder was yet a man. At the bottom of his heart he had compassion for Dermott for he secretly believed Dermott was innocent. But this compassion could not release Dermott from his misery.

Dermott, made a pious call to God. He entreated Jesus daily and promised to deliver things he was unsure he could deliver, if only he were freed early and above all else, had his name cleared. He wanted the world to know that he had been 'set up' by the church and its superiors. This was the church in which he had placed his trust, pledged his life to and prison had been his reward. He endeavoured to convince himself that it was man who had caused his misery and not Jesus. One day, not now, but a long way in the future, God would punish these evil beings.

Dermott heard from the recesses of his cell the noises made by the preparations for receiving him. He guessed something uncommon was happening, as it was not a visiting day. He had ceased to have any meaningful intercourse with the world because he looked upon himself as mentally dead. The door opened and an old priest appeared next to the warder.

'Good evening my son, forgive me for not having come before but I have been on a sabbatical. How are you?'

'Save for wanting my freedom and understanding why God has allowed this terrible event to unfold, I am fine,' and the words came out so slowly and in a tone so melancholy, that the old priest feared that the devil himself had uttered them.

'Has your family been to visit you yet?'

'No, I won't allow it. I do not wish them to see this dreadful place, it is full of lunatics! I am the only sane person here apart from the warders and the governor.'

'Well it is not for me to comment, I am here to offer counselling on behalf of the authorities and the church.'

'The church, ah yes, the church. Would that be the same church that arranged for me to come here by default? Or to be nearer to the truth, by the deliberate arrangement of father guardian. He is a member of the queers' club too? Listen father, the rector, the police and the jury say I am guilty of sexual assault, so if they say so, it must be true.'

'My poor boy, I am not here to take sides and your case does sound incredulous. Would you like to pray with me?'

'Father, praying no longer appeals to me, I am no longer sure that I believe in God. I offered my whole life to him and now I find myself lost, alone, falsely accused and without hope. It seems to me that those who follow the Devil's path are on the path paved with gold. While those who follow the Lord are travelling on the path of unhappiness.'

'My son, I can understand that, but remember that God works in mysterious ways, I feel sure you will find peace at the end of this dreadful affair. Let me pray for you instead.' The old priest's eyes were so gentle and love and kindness beamed from his face. Towards the end of the recital, thick tears rolled down Dermott's cheeks as he listened intently to the words of the kind old man.

'My son, your tears are the greatest reward God could have sent me today and I will pray that you find peace and contentment soon. Forgive those who have made you suffer so much.' And the gentleness in his voice touched Dermott's soul. But an instant later, all Dermott's misfortunes came leaping back to his mind and he let forth a tirade of abuse about everything and everyone he could think of, that had caused him to suffer so much, in such a short time.

'I can never forgive them, they are evil, all of them. When I get out of this God-forsaken hole, I will have my revenge. Just watch them fall, one by one'. And in his mind he conjured up such imaginable horrors for his victims that even the devil himself would have turned in fear.

'You say that now, my son, but as time passes, your anger will subside.' A few moments later, the old priest knocked on the cell door, asked to be led out, and then disappeared down the passage.

The days were long and the nights even longer and Dermott struggled to come to terms with his situation. He had to find a means of restoring lucidity and clearness of mind for he truly was in a dismal state. Those in whom he had placed his trust had let him down badly. The counselling he received did nothing to appease his state of mind and he renewed his vow to punish those who had wronged him. But most of all, he was angry, angry with the God who had allowed such misfortune to fall upon him. He began to question his motives for wanting to join the priesthood. He asked himself. Can I have been tracing a false path? Can the end which I proposed, be a mistaken end? Has my pursuit to become a man of the cloth been a sacrilegious undertaking? He felt his position was like that of a person wounded in a dream; he could feel the wound but could not recollect when he had received it.

The weeks turned into months and Dermott had exhausted all human resources. He was still a young man aged 21 but he *felt* considerably older. In one final attempt to restore his morale and his faith, he prayed and prayed aloud. He laid every action of his life before the almighty, proposed tasks to accomplish, and at the end of every prayer, introduced the entreaty oftener addressed to man than to God, 'Forgive us our trespasses as we forgive those that trespass against us.' Yet in spite of all his prayers, he found no solace. Then a gloomy feeling took possession of him. He clung to one idea that of his happiness, destroyed without apparent cause by at least four evil men. Rage succeeded this. He uttered blasphemies that made his warder recoil with horror, dashed himself against the walls of his cell, attacked everything, and the least little thing that annoyed him. He then devoted his persecutors to the most horrible tortures he could imagine, and found them all insufficient, because after torture came death, and after death if not repose, at least that insensibility that resembles it. The judge had been correct with his decision that was for sure, a psychiatric prison, for a psychiatric prisoner, because he felt sure he was becoming slightly mad. And by constantly dwelling on these negative thoughts, he felt a slight twist in his mind. He was definitely travelling on the wrong path; the path paved with gold seemed to be leading in the opposite direction.

Chapter Nine

Slumber would not visit Dermott's eyes easily for his mind was still focused on the *path* into the early hours of the morning. He had great difficulty in riding this subject from his mind. The light came flooding into his cell; it was Friday once more. Was this to be a Good Friday? It was an exercise day followed by recreational activities. The mobile library would be visiting today. He would make another visit to this library, looking for books of a factual nature. He never looked at non-fictional titles, it was just not in his make-up. He was only interested in factual titles, anything, which he considered, related to true life. Recreation time had arrived and he waited patiently as the mobile library visited the first two cellblocks. By the time it reached his own, he had lost interest and couldn't be bothered to put any effort into selecting a suitable title. He was just about to walk away empty handed when the librarian noticed the look of disinterest on his features.

'Hey Dermott, we have some new titles today that we have not had time to sort onto the shelves. Take a look through these.'

'Okay, thanks,' and he began to casually sort through the books. Out of the dozen or so new books he picked up one or two but then replaced them as insignificant trivia. He was just about to walk away when a thick paperback caught his eye. It was the gaudy colour and the almost obscene picture on the cover, which had caused it to stand out from others on the shelf. The cover frontispiece depicted a picture of 'The Devil' a naked half man half beast complete with scaly black skin, horns, tail, and cloven hoof. The picture was intended to display 'The Devil' as a phallic symbol and it most certainly achieved its purpose. Dermott examined the title 'A Biography of the Devil'. He thought this would be a book of mundane fiction and replaced it on the shelf about to disregard it as 'trash' when he noticed the author's name Carl Jung. He picked up the book again and read the sleeve notes transfixed, as if he had found the key to his own personal vault of gold.

'My God,' he mumbled, 'this is a sort of treatise on Satan.' He immediately walked up to the librarian and had his book stamped and retired to the quiet part of the room to commence his studies.

For some strange reason he now had a renewed vigour and the satanic demons which came to haunt him from time to time disappeared into the void. He may have been born on 6-6-1966, but for now at least that fact did not appear to trouble him. He was not sure why he was reading this book or indeed what he hoped to find. He just felt he had to read it. Maybe it was his subconscious guiding him or was it a trick of the devil to get him to read it? By the time he had reached the fourth chapter he was absorbed. Was he in a dream or was he awake?

Jung referred to the Devil as a servant of God. The tempter of human mankind. God and the Devil were two sides of the same coin. Each one of us has a shadow running in tandem with our good side. Jung continued. How can I be substantial if I fail to cast a shadow? I must have a dark side if I am to be whole. Without darkness, light has no definition! All this was music to his ears. Perhaps he thought; each and every one of us has a dark side. Maybe we are all servants of God and the Devil simultaneously. If that was the case, then was being born on 6-6-66 significant or not? Carl Jung was no 20th century novelist. He was, in his time, a very intelligent being, acclaimed the world over. A disciple of Freud. His narrative was considered to be the gospel in some quarters.

Dermott began to ask himself once more why he was the innocent victim of such a despicable crime.

His tormentors must have been acting as the dark side of the coin, but that was even worse as they were living in the house of God. No, he just could not get his brain around it all. Most people, he convinced himself, were innately good. He examined his conscience as if checking himself. He decided he did not really have a wish to harm anyone (save his accusers) and therefore, his first thoughts must have been correct. The majority of people are blessed with a kind and caring nature.

By the time the evening arrived, he had absorbed so much information that his mind continued to whirr deep into the next morning. He seemed unable to settle. He was dissecting every piece of information back and forth, to and fro, and still he came to no conclusion. He once more subjected his persecutors to the most horrible tortures he could imagine and then finally, in the early hours, mentally exhausted and on the verge of sleep, he remembered invoking the great tempter. As Jesus has abandoned me, and you are also a servant of God, I want you to get me out of this mess. When he awoke in the morning he was unable to remember what had been thoughts and what had been dreams. And as the months slipped by, the pages of the book were so imprinted on his mind that he knew the contents inside out.

Chapter Ten

The next morning rose dull and cloudy, which seemed to fit perfectly with Dermott's melancholy state. The warder entered once more. 'Dermott, report to the governor's office after breakfast would you he wishes to see you.'

'Do you know what it is about?'

'Don't rightly know, asked me to send you up there, that is all I was told.'

Dermott was ushered into the governor's room where he found the governor seated and talking to a man of about 50, tall, portly and imposing with a massive, strongly marked face and a commanding figure. He was also well cut in a black outfit, which told the world he was a man of the cloth. Dermott recognised him as the Archbishop. He stared at Dermott who was so fixed with a look of grief and despair in his eyes that the Archbishop's smile was turned in an instant to horror and pity.

'You have come to inform me I need more counselling, have you not?' said Dermott.

'No, Dermott, but I have some news to impart to you.'

'No doubt you think me mad.'

'Well no, Dermott, but I see that you have some great trouble and a torrid time.'

'God knows I have! – a trouble which is enough to unseat my reason. Public disgrace I can handle although I am a man whose character had until now never born a stain. But this matter is a public and private affliction and in so frightful a form that it has been enough to shake my very soul.'

'Please compose yourself, Dermott. The news I have for you may help you come to terms with some of the dreadful events that have overtaken you.'

'Nothing can resolve the happenings of late. I have been abandoned by everyone, including God.'

'Dermott, brother Sean wishes to be allowed to visit you.' Dermott's jaw dropped. Had a burning chasm opened before his eyes, he could not have been more stupefied.

'What would that evil one want with me? If I could summon all the love in the whole wide world, he would never be forgiven – never.'

'Dermott, I can see how you are suffering but will you not at least listen to what he has to say? I will be in attendance if you allow the visit.'

'And what good would it serve?'

'Dermott, I know he has something important to say to you. Will you not give him two minutes and hear him out?'

'One minute only, but keep him at the other end of the room and tell him there will be no forgiveness.'

'Bless you, Dermott, I will arrange it for next Thursday, same time.'

The following Thursday Dermott was seated at the desk with the Archbishop. From down the corridor he could hear the sound of the double doors swinging open and then the noise of what sounded like a squeaky wheelbarrow whose wheel needed oiling.

30 seconds later, a gaunt and haggard man was pushed into the office in a wheelchair. It was Sean. But it was not the Sean that Dermott remembered. This man had aged considerably. His face was lined and he looked meagre and sickly. His breathing was laboured and he was wheezing badly. Dermott gazed in astonishment at the transformation that had taken place in the countenance of Sean. He looked liked a wizened old man. Sean tried to speak but struggled with some difficulty.

'I have come to see you because I have something to share with you. I am dy- dying. I have an incurable disease. I need to seek your forgiveness if that is possible. I have been punis- punished by the almighty above.' Dermott's anger began to rise but at the same time he was consumed by a feeling of contentment, looking at the sickly specimen of a human being. He felt as if he had been slightly avenged for all his sufferings. But at no time at all did he feel any compassion for the instigator of the crime and therefore the most guilty.

'I do not really understand why you have come here. The only way you can help me is by retracting your lies and clearing my name.'

'Dermott, I need your forgiveness I am dying.'

'And I am dying of a broken heart and a broken soul. Clear my name and I might consider it.'

'Dermott, the almighty has punished me. I now have that terrible illness AIDS. Will you forgive me?'

Dermott was now consumed by an even greater feeling of contentment as if he were controlling events to his own satisfaction. But at the same time he felt slightly uneasy.

'Are you going to clear my name or not?'

'I will, I will, just give me your pardon.'

'What are you going to do for me first?'

'I will clear it all with the authorities. Archbishop, you can be a witness to these events. Will you take it all down? Dermott, a few years ago, as a relatively young man, I began to suffer with severe pains in my joints. An uncommon occurrence for one so young. Then I broke an ankle in a bizarre accident and I began to think that this was God's way of warning me without actually striking me down. I ignored these warnings, squandered the gifts I had been granted and through selfish greed, coveted the things I wanted in life instead of earning them in a proper fashion. Then I was diagnosed with this dreadful disease and then I realised it was God who was punishing me. And now it is far too late and there is no point of return for me and I wish to make my peace with you and the world. Dermott, I have wronged you badly and I want the world to know you are innocent of the accusations levelled at you.' Dermott was totally transfixed as he listened to this recital with great intensity.

'Archbishop, I wish the world to know that Dermott is innocent of all the charges levelled against him. It has all been a terrible mistake.'

'It seems as if I am hearing the recital to a dream. But I have seen things so extraordinary, that what you refer to now seems less astonishing,' said Dermott with an ironical smile. And as he uttered his comment he recalled how he had asked the 'devil' to intercede for him in his hour of need and once more he renewed his vow of vengeance to punish his calumniators. And later that same day, the Archbishop set the wheels in motion to procure Dermott's release because he knew that the wheels of justice turned very slowly when a man was innocent. Dermott had very little intercourse with the outside world and absorbed himself in his books and periodicals. Lying on his bed, he thumbed through a supplement of a Sunday newspaper. The supplement consisted of an article on Astrology and another one on Numerology. It was this second one that caught his eye. He began reading with intense concentration, his imagination fired by his satanic leanings. The article referred to Numerology readings, suggesting that every human being was governed by his own particular set of numbers. He could not put it down. The article offered a free 'reading' at the Britannia Hotel, Liverpool during one of the 'mystical evenings' in exchange for an annual subscription fee of £50, which entitled one to a regular delivery of the monthly periodical. If and when he got out of this mess, he would take up the offer forthwith.

Chapter Eleven

About three days after the visit from Sean, Dermott was summoned to the governor's office once more. 'Dermott, there is a request from your mother to visit you before your release. I realise you have declined all previous requests of this nature but as you will be leaving here in the not too distant future, I wondered if you would change your mind on this occasion.'

'Governor, I have told you before, no visitors.'

'Says she wants to bring someone along with her, someone named Teresa.' A blush of embarrassment mounted Dermott's features upon hearing this name, the name he had uttered in his most private moments. 'Teresa, well I may consider............' and Dermott's voice trailed off stifled with emotion.

'Then I have only to make the arrangements for the visit,' replied the governor.

Dermott raised his eyes to heaven and he knew he would have to prepare his courage, for never would he need it more. Teresa, Teresa, he thought about the times he had uttered her name. With a sigh of melancholy, with a groan of sorrow, with a last effort of despair; he had uttered it consumed with heat, frozen with cold and now he had an opportunity to see her face once more and to be surrounded by the warmth of her spontaneity.

The day of the visit had arrived and the morning sun rose clear and resplendent, gilding the heavens with its bright refulgent beams.

Dermott was seated nonchalantly glancing at a newspaper when Shelagh appeared at the door. For a second, he thought she was alone but then he spied a second figure in the background. A slim attractive woman with beautiful bone structure and eyes sparkling with the vitality of youth stared across at Dermott. He gazed transfixed at the beauty of this young female form. It was his beloved, Teresa. There was a strange silence, no one daring to speak and then first Shelagh and then Teresa extended their arms and embraced Dermott with feelings of boundless love. Shelagh spoke first.

'Dermott my boy, this dreadful affair will soon be over thank God and all the misfortunes will be past.'

'My misfortunes will soon be passed but punishment will fall upon the perpetrators of this sham, in fact, the first punishment has already been meted out.'

'Punishment Dermott, what punishment? How can you talk so despairingly when God has answered all our prayers.'

An involuntary shiver passed over Dermott's whole frame and one overriding thought raced into his already overloaded mind; had it been God or Beelzebub, his newly formed acquaintance, that had commenced the punishments. He could no longer remember.

'Mother, one of my persecutors is dying of AIDS and it is only a matter of time before Providence strikes the others.'

'Dermott, how can you say such things? You talk as if you are Providence itself.'

'Mother I have been wronged, humiliated before the whole world and taken away from my loved ones. I shall have my revenge.'

And as he said these words, both Teresa and his mother gazed upon Dermott's manly countenance on which grief and hatred still impressed a threatening impression. Teresa spoke next with an accent of despair. 'Dermott, I know you could not have done those awful things of which you were accused, but perhaps you will be able to forgive in time.' Dermott fearing to yield to the entreaties of her he so ardently loved recalled his sufferings to the assistance of his hatred. 'Not exact vengeance on those accursed specimens. Abandon my purpose when I am about to see its accomplishment. Never!'

'Revenge yourself, then, Dermott,' cried his poor mother, 'but do not get into any further bother. Let *God's* vengeance fall on the culprits, not your *own*.' Then both Shelagh and Teresa chose a comfortable position, for listening to the painful recital they expected to hear. Dermott moved his seat into a corner of the room, where he himself would be in deep shadow, while the light would be fully thrown on the listeners. Then with head bent down and hands clasped or rather clenched together, he commenced his narration. The two ladies gave him their whole attention and Dermott paused only once or twice to answer the most delicate of questions. When Dermott had finished his tale, he placed his hand on his crucifix and added the words, 'I swear to you both by my soul's salvation and my faith as a Christian, I have told everything to you as it occurred, and as the angel of men will tell it to the ear of God at the day of the last judgement.' Shelagh spoke next. 'Well I think we have heard enough, let us talk about happier times to come.'

Then Teresa gazed intently at her hero with a look that radiated both warmth and pity.

'I hope you are coming to visit me as soon as you leave this awful place,' and she pronounced these words with an accent of such intense warmth, that Dermott could not restrain a sob. The lion was daunted; the avenger was conquered. Before he could answer, Shelagh interjected with one of her usual motherly pearls of wisdom. 'Dermott, my son, I have prepared your room for the homecoming. I take it you are moving back home at least for the time being, that is.'

'Well just for a few weeks until I have sorted out my life.'

'Will you be going back to the college in due course?'

'No, I have applied for a post at the university hoping to use my degree in chemistry and biology,' and then, wanting it to appear as an afterthought, he added, 'Will you be still there, Teresa?' But before she could answer, Shelagh answered for her.

'Teresa will be away home by then, won't you?'

'You can drop me a line Dermott, I will leave the address with Shelagh.'

'Fine, be sure to do so.'

After Teresa and his mother had left, a gloomy shadow seemed to overspread everything. Around him and within him the flight of thought appeared stopped; his mind slumbered, as does the body after extreme fatigue. He was thinking, thinking about Teresa and the secret he had yet to unravel. It was his intention to set to work on this project, just as soon as it was practicable.

And as for Shelagh, although her ambitions for Dermott had now disappeared into oblivion, she took some inwardly comfort, from knowing her son would probably obtain the post at the university. He held a *first* in biology and chemistry and had a reputation as owning a razor sharp mind, to accompany his academic qualifications. Indeed, he had been tipped to become a leading light in the forensic world before he chose to study for the priesthood.

A brisk North easterly wind was blowing sleet into Dermott's face as he stepped out of the taxi; but this only encouraged him to push his face into full force of the elements; because this was his first day of freedom, since he was taken to the dreadful asylum 12 months previously. He announced he was taking a break until he took up his new post at university, in the next term. The priestly life he had decided was not for him after all. Firstly, he was too attracted to the female form to remain celibate. Secondly, he now felt the church was a hypocritical institution and of course he still wanted his vengeance, he would not forget that. Thirdly, and especially since he had read Jung's book, he still had those nagging doubts that he was in league with the fallen angel. Since the visit from Sean, he had continued to feel he was acting out his role of punisher and he was determined to crush his persecutors, no matter how long the task took. But before he put that on his agenda he had other unfinished business to tend to. It was now, his third week of freedom.

Walking into the foyer of the Britannia Hotel (Liverpool), he looked for the notice board displaying the events. Sure enough, he found what he was looking for 'A mystical evening with Petulingro 7pm – Embassy Suite'.

Unsure as to what to expect, he felt rather nervous and conspicuous as he entered the room, which consisted of a stage, seating down the middle of the room and eight or nine display units round the side of the room. The display units offered a choice of subjects ranging from fortune telling with a crystal ball, tarot card reading, palm reading, tea leaf readings and at the very end, Numerology readings. Dermott shuffled along to the end and a female dressed in what looked like a gypsy outfit sat at a desk, behind which were display boards with strange symbols stuck to them looking like stars and numbers with their ends chopped off.

The woman in the gypsy outfit spoke.

'Good evening to you young sir, can I be of assistance?'

'Yes, I have been reading several articles on numerology and I have become quite fascinated by the subject. Can you enlighten me a little further?'

'Well, if you subscribe to our monthly publication for a minimum of one year, you will be entitled not only to the monthly publication but also a free reading here this evening, before the start of the main show which commences at 9pm, with Petulingro herself. If you sign up for the subscription this evening, you will receive an introductory discount of £15. The total cost including the reading will be £35. How does that sound?'

'Well, I can't stay for the whole evening anyway, so that sounds all right to me.' And Dermott sat down before the old woman with mixed feeling of scepticism and intense interest.

'Now, first things first. I need your first name and date of birth.' When Dermott heard her ask for his date of birth he felt the tension inside him start to rise. He wondered what sort of comment would come next as he rattled off his name and date of birth. He half expected a reference to Beelzebub or Satan to follow, but nothing sinister followed. The old woman began writing down numbers that were somehow related to Dermott's Christian name and that was followed by her writing down 6-6-1966 and then inverting these numbers so that they read 9961-9-9. She totalled the first set of numbers 6-6-1966=34 then the second set 9961-9-9=43 then she carried out a calculation 3+4=7 and then 4+3=7. Then next she subtracted 34 from 43=9.

She paused as if checking her calculations for errors and then she let out an exclamation.

'Heavens above, I have never seen a more pronounced and definitive set of numbers. These are most singular. Would you like me to explain them?' And as she spoke, Dermott noticed she had become ashen faced.

'Yes, please go ahead.'

'Well, I have never seen a set like this before. You will note, that whichever way we look at them, the correct way up, or inverted, they total the same on both occasions. The number that remains is 7 in both instances.

Now, if we count to the seventh letter of the alphabet, that is G. Now the letter G in numerology represents God.' Upon hearing this, Dermott was shaken and he felt his heart race faster. He took a swig of water from the tumbler and tried not to look flustered.

'This is one of the strongest signs in the numerological index and it means you carry genes that make your chosen path in life almost infallible. Does that make any sense to you or shall I elaborate in greater detail?'

'No, no it makes a great deal of sense, you don't need you to elaborate.'

'Also, if we subtract the total of your numbers 34 from the inverted version, we arrive at 9. The ninth letter of the alphabet is 'I' and stands for immune in the numerological index. These are truly, a strong set of numbers that will enable you to achieve your desires and ambitions in life. Shall I continue?'

Dermott was completely taken in and mesmerised by now.

'Yes, please go on.'

'Well as a precautionary note, we always look at your main weakness so as to help you guard against this throughout you life. This gives you a true insight, into the type of person you are, and if you guard against this trait you should have nothing to worry about. So, looking at your name Dermott, we have the following :

D   E   R   M   O   T   T
4   5 18 13 15 20 20 = 95

The corresponding number of the alphabet represents each letter of your name and therefore the total for your name is 95. 9-5 =4. With *this* equation, we subtract the numbers, because we are looking at your major weakness. The fourth letter of the numerological index is D and this is normally associated with deviousness or deceit. So Dermott, it is highly likely that your major weakness will be connected to these elements and you should guard against that if that is the case.'

Dermott was having real trouble concealing his agitated state, so near to the knuckle had this wizened old woman reached. His face had coloured up and she sensed his discomfort. Being used to dealing with this sort of situation, she tried to make him feel better by saying.

'Remember, Dermott, we only suggest your guard against this as your main weakness. It is more of help really.'

'Yes, thank you, it has been a most interesting reading. Here is the money for my subscription and the address to send it to. I have to be going now as I am short of time, thank you.'

A week later he tackled his second problem.

Dermott wandered into the reference library hoping to investigate the mystery surrounding Teresa.

'Excuse me, could you tell me where I can find the birth records for this area?'

'I am sorry, but we don't hold records here; they are held centrally in London. You would have to go to St Catherine's house.' Dermott was slightly taken aback by this new finding, for London seemed a long way off. He would have to put his plans on hold for a short while. Stepping outside onto the pavement he had to avoid colliding with a young beautiful woman with a dazzling appearance, who was so pre-occupied with her haste that she failed to notice any of the passers by. This event stirred Dermott into action and he followed her with his eagle eye, as she hastily crossed the road trying to attract the attention of two people who appeared to be waiting for someone to arrive. Upon reaching the two people, she sprang forward extending her open arms to embrace first one figure then the other. For a moment, Dermott thought it was his imagination playing tricks with his mind. He gazed across at the three people now engaged in endearing conversation. Instantly he recognised the tall portly shape of the male; it was none other than father guardian! He scrutinised the older woman to establish if he knew her and as his mind unlocked the vaults a name came into his thoughts. Yes, he recognised her also. It was Mary Murphy one of the parishioners at his local church! Mary was a very good looking woman with beauty only surpassed now by that of her daughter Helen, the young lady who had just rushed by him. He watched with prying eyes at these three people who now moved slowly out of the precinct. He followed them from a safe distance hoping they would not turn round. But he need not have worried because they were engrossed in their own world to the exclusion it seemed of everyone else. Dermott remained for nearly quarter of an hour perfectly hidden by the shadows of the buildings, which formed the shopping centre, but by a sort of instinctive impulse, he withdrew when he saw the priest occasionally turning around as if to check whether or not they were being followed. Then they turned into a side street where at the corner stood a small coffee shop and Dermott had to halt for fear of being discovered. He carefully watched his prey and strained his ears to catch a word for they were now standing outside examining the tariff in the window. He was unsure as to what he expected to hear but he listened all the same.

'Well Bernard, shall we go inside or not?' It was Mary who spoke.

'Yes, it looks most suitable, what do you think Helen?'

'Looks fine to me Father,' Helen replied. Dermott moved a pace or two nearer hoping to catch more of the conversation but the noise of the traffic drowned out all possibility of further eavesdropping. And to move another step nearer would invite discovery. They moved into the café and Dermott was left to ponder on his findings.

He was once more left with a mystery and this also he wanted to solve. The burning question was; Why was his old rector out with Mary and Helen Murphy? He could not let this lie as he had a score to settle with the rector. A very big score.

Helen had used the word 'Father' quite distinctly. 'It looks fine to me Father' he could not get the words out of his head. But of course this could easily have been a term of reference, after all he was a priest. And now the cunning came into Dermott's mind as he now had two reasons to make a visit to St Catherine's house.

Chapter Twelve

Dermott arrived at the famous building on a hot and sticky morning and he was amazed at the number of people scratching around at such an early hour. He was brimming with excitement and gazed with fascination, upon the row of volumes stacked neatly upon the shelves. It was hard for him to take in that so many people were doing something very similar. Everyone seemed to be jotting down notes and he surmised that they must have been looking up their family trees. Some of these folk were dressed in formal suits and looked very officious and he wondered what *they* were doing there. Dermott scanned the shelves for the volume he wanted. He found the births section and set to work. The information looked scant and it was.

He found the section pertaining to Murray and now he searched meticulously the records for the month of August 1968. But after half an hour, he had to admit defeat for he could find no reference to anyone named Teresa Murray having a mother named Shelagh. He wondered if the information he was seeking was held at the GRO in Dublin, for there were no clues held in the volumes of this building.

He was becoming despondent so now was the time to switch his search to a different volume. He wondered how old Helen Murphy could be. About 23 he surmised, so he decided to make a sweep of the volumes starting with the year 1960 and ending with 1967. The records for 1960-1966 yielded nothing, but in the third quarter for 1967 was a reference relating to a Mary Murphy and a daughter named Helen. Unfortunately, there were three other entries with the same names so he scrutinised the districts for each entry and one of them referred to Liverpool. Surely this had to be the correct one! He copied the information onto a form and handed it together with the fee to the cashier. Now the waiting game had set in and it would be another three or four days, before he would know if he had any evidence with which to work. He set off for the long journey back North. Three days later, an envelope dropped onto the mat and Dermott retired to his room, to open the letter. He extracted the document carefully, the pink texture of the paper reflecting strongly against the fluorescent lighting. He stared at the neatly hand written text and thanked his God for revealing this vital piece of information.

It read ;

Where Born – Rainhill, Liverpool

When Born – 20th July 1967

Name (if any) - Helen

Sex - Girl

Name, surname and maiden name of Mother:

    Mary Murphy *formerly* White

Name and surname of Father

    Bernard Brunton

Signature, description and residence of informant:

    Mary Murphy *formerly* White, Mother, Booth Street, Turvey, Liverpool.

When Registered – 5th August 1967

Sigtnature of Redistrar – P Rowland

So now he had a hold over another of his enemies. Bernard had fathered a love child. At that moment as he was thinking how he would use this information, his thoughts were interrupted by another more overpowering thought. He seemed to be receiving assistance from an unexpected quarter, the Devil himself. For one brief second, he felt as if he had a new-found power but then he dismissed this as a matter of coincidence. His main persecutor had been punished and now he could avenge himself on a second. But was it the help of the Devil or was it luck? He was unsure at present.

He thought about how to exact his revenge and for one fleeting moment, wondered if he should show compassion. But this thought was about as strong as a dwarf about to enter into combat with Hercules.

Once more, dark storm clouds were boiling up in the afternoon sky and a cold sweat broke out over Dermott's brow as he entered the pay phone booth. He dialled the number and a cheery voice answered.

'Newsroom, Don Rathbone speaking.'

'Hi there, I have some information about the rector of St Ambrose's seminary, which I think you will find very interesting.'

'What exactly is it?'

'I think you will find very newsworthy, he is the father of a lovechild.' There was a pause and then the voice interjected.

'Well, can you substantiate these allegations and who are you?'

'Check your mail tomorrow the evidence will be sent to you this afternoon,' and with that Dermott, replaced the handset. He stepped outside, walked over to the post box and dropped the damning documents into the mailbox. The following day, he scoured the early editions for evidence of his dirty work. Nothing could he find. Perhaps the envelope had not yet arrived. At 4.30 he was walking through the city centre and it was then that he caught sight of a newspaper placard.

It read in bold letters; SHAME OF HIGH RANKING PRIEST and it was then that Dermott knew he had become an adversary of the devil.

I was seven o'clock at night on the 21st of June 1988. One might have thought already that God's curse hung over a degenerate world, for there was an awesome hush and a felling of vague expectancy in the sultry and stagnant air. The sun had long set, but one blood red gash like an open wound lay low in the distant West. The story had now filtered through to the local television screens, sketchy, but nevertheless sufficiently powerful to have done the damage.

In the residence of the Archbishop, frantic words were being exchanged between the hierarchy of the Diocese.

'I don't care how clean his past reputation has been, there is evidence here for the world to see and he *has* to go.'

'But he has worked so hard and tirelessly in this community and you were about to bestow him as a Monsignor.'

'That was before this lot unfolded,' screamed the Bishop at the same time shaking a bundle of papers in his hand.

'My decision is final. He is to be posted to the Primate in Ireland. He can serve his days out as a parish priest!'

And with this outburst, the meeting came rapidly to a close.

Chapter Thirteen

Dermott began to take stock of his situation. He seemed to have risen from the depths of despair to a situation where life was far more bearable than it had been in recent times. It now seemed to him that if he was not yet master of his own destiny at least he was beginning to take some control over matters, which had previously been beyond his control. He was becoming resilient and determined to triumph over adversity. His thoughts began to stray and he examined the events that had unfolded since the day he had picked up the book written by Jung.

Was he now an agent being led on by an invisible force or was he being driven on out of anger and hatred? He examined the past and the present and then endeavoured to pierce futurity. The most dreadful misfortunes, the most frightful sufferings, the abandonment of all those who loved him, formed the trials of his youth; when suddenly from captivity, solitude and misery he had now been restored to light and liberty. Now he felt driven on like an exterminating angel. Was his role to mete out punishment to his persecutors, those who had offended Deity? It seemed the more he became revengeful, cunning, and wicked, the more he overcame every obstacle and reached the goal. A sinister smile passed over Dermott's lips and he shouted out the words, 'Woe to those who meet me in my career for I am a divine instrument of the devil and I shall have my just rewards.' And with wickedness in his heart he began to examine ways of dealing with Patrick and Michael.

Since the time of Sean's confession (who was now at death's door) both Patrick Mahoney and Michael Flanders had been interviewed, arrested and then released once more. The likelihood that they would face charges of perjury was relatively strong. It was up to the police to build a sound enough case. Of course, Dermott wanted his own retribution and was determined to act as judge, jury and executioner.

Dermott's work at the university had drifted his concentration away from vengeance for a while and he had still not got round writing to Teresa. The chemistry department was the largest single unit at the university followed by the biology department. Dermott headed up both. Toxicology was one of the busiest departments of the chemistry laboratory, and Dermott's work was divided between the twin menaces drugs and poisons. But he also spent 60 percent of his time working on viruses or to be exact, he was in charge of a small team hoping to find a cure for the most deadliest of them all, the AIDS virus. How ironic that he should be leading an investigation into the weapon that had wiped out the guiltiest, of his enemies!

As the university representative, he was in close collaboration with the National Institutes of Health, world-wide.

The greatest brains in the world exchanged information on the subject on a regular basis. Documents, theses, theories and all manner of articles, passed from one Institute to another on a monthly cycle. Dermott was called upon to deliver a detailed lecture to the British Medical Council and began describing the virus as such;

'If I were a devil creating a malicious virus to cause the most problems for the human race, the virus would be AIDS. The virus has found the Achilles' heel of the immune system.'

He continued.

'Why is that so? Well, to begin with, HIV primarily attacks T cells, white blood cells that play a major role in the body's immune response to invasion by viruses and other infectious agents. It is the T cells that directly attack infected or malignant body cells, while at the same time helping to orchestrate deployment of other immune-system tactics, such as the production of antibodies. And HIV specifically goes after the very T cells-called T4, or *helper T cells* that do the most to facilitate these functions and activate as well another kind of white blood cells called the *natural killer cells*. These cells, like T cells, patrol the body, killing infected cells on contact. The killer cells bind fast to their targets and deliver a lethal dose of toxic chemicals that bore holes in the infected cells' membranes. Thus perforated, the cells leak out their fluids and soon burst. So, knock out T4 cells and you knock out a big chunk of the body's immune response. It's a masterful and insidious strategy.'

He paused to take a glass of water, the audience transfixed with the accuracy and perfection of his delivery. One could hear a pin drop. Dermott continued.

'But that is not all. For HIV also attacks macrophages, another one of the indispensable characters of the immune system. Macrophages are scavenger white cells that roam the body engulfing foreign matter and cellular debris. They also play an important part in initiating immune response in the first place, as they alert the T cells that there is an invasion to be fought. So by infecting the macrophages, HIV further debilitates the immune system. At the same time, infected macrophages spread the virus throughout the body, as these scavenger cells don't quickly die of infection, as do T cells. They continue travelling the body, now bearing an unwelcome burden of HIV. In fact, these circulating, infected microphages may be the vehicle by which HIV causes the neurological difficulties often seen in AIDS. Loss of memory, failing judgement, and declining bodily co-ordination during the course of the disease may be the results of macrophages carrying their deadly cargo to the brain.

'So HIV's attack strategy is far more sophisticated and clever than that of any other human virus; it debilitates the immune system itself. It disarms the body, not overwhelming it from without but by infiltrating it from within. Yet, crippled as it is, the immune system still has resources to fight the virus - if it could find the invader. For not content with simply disabling the immune system, HIV is also a master at hiding from it. Other than the capricious influenza virus, there is no other virus as adept as HIV at changing the configuration of its surface so as to elude immune detection. HIV mutates incredibly rapidly, often within the very person it infects; there have been instances of viruses in the same individual varying by as much as 30 percent. The idea here is old, and effective, as espionage; if you can't find me you won't stop me.

'Ladies and gentlemen, let us unite to find a cure. You know where I can be contacted.'

There was a two second silence when Dermott had finished speaking, as if the audience where in anticipation of more to come. But when they realised that he had finished speaking, a raucous applause ensued and cheer upon cheer rent the roof. The Chairman of the British Medical Council gave a very sincere vote of thanks to Dermott for such an informative and detailed report and almost instantaneously, Dermott rose to great prominence in the medical world.

Chapter Fourteen

Dermott was seated in his chair in his laboratory and was warming his hands on the radiators for a sharp frost had set in and outside the windows were thick with ice crystals. It was March again. His colleague, Bradstreet, who was in the habit of opening the early morning mail remarked, 'Dermott, there is an interesting communication from the Boston Institute of Medicine arrived this morning. A guy named Francis Pepper has been working on trying to produce a vaccine against AIDS. It is early days, but says he has had some success with mice and wants to do a trial, with selected cases, in both Boston and the UK. He would like you to read his notes and contact him.'

Dermott picked up the bundle of papers with a casual indifference, for he had been down this road many times before. Regularly, he received communications from this doctor or that doctor, all claiming they had unravelled the mystery surrounding the AIDS virus. But it had always been to no avail. All research led up a blind ally.

He glanced up and down the first couple of pages and then something caught his eye, and by the time he had reached page three, he was engrossed. Pepper was claiming that he had grown the AIDS virus successfully and that he had developed a technique to identify antibodies, to the virus in the blood, of HIV infected mice. He now wanted to test this on humans but before he did so, he wanted Dermott to substantiate these findings.

It was March and Dermott painstakingly set to work to find the guilty virus. By May, he was convinced that Pepper's findings were on the right lines and he confirmed as such both to Pepper and the British Medical Council. He requested of the latter for funds to be made available for further research, but more importantly insisted that a trial be initiated for infected humans. He suggested that this pilot exercise should become the basis for a screening test to monitor blood donations. The British Medical Council were not slow in coming forward. They could see nothing but good publicity from this even if it meant sharing the limelight with other students of the subject thousands of miles away. The British Medical Council hastily arranged for Dermott to publish four papers in the science magazine to describe his results.

It was a blazing hot day in June. The laboratory was like an oven and the glare of the sunlight upon the windows was painful to the eye. It was hard to believe that this was the same laboratory, which loomed so gloomily through the fogs and cold of winter. The blinds were half drawn and Dermott sat at a desk reading and re-reading a letter, which he had received through the morning post. Dermott was too absorbed for conversation but suddenly his voice broke in upon Bradstreet's thoughts.

'You were right, Douglas, the government has now agreed to a trial for infected humans commencing in three months time. A list of ten volunteer patients is to follow along with their comprehensive medical history. A similar programme is to be conducted simultaneously in Boston. Looks like we are going to be busy.'

Dermott was poring over some papers when he first heard the fax machine flicker into life. He glanced casually over to the one or two papers, which were now tumbling from the machine onto the floor. From the distance he was seated he could see the British Medical Council insignia on the top of the first page, which was now lying face upwards on the laboratory floor. He walked over to the papers, picked them up examining them as he did so. It contained a list of names and addresses. It was obvious that the information therein contained details of the ten volunteers, who were about to act as trialists for the British Medical Council. Dermott began to meticulously scrutinise the information. Suddenly, he was seized by an uncontrollable fit of trembling and at the same time, he let out a burst of maniacal laughter, enough to instil fear into the mind of anyone listening. But the room was empty save Dermott and therefore, no one was witness to the spectacle that had just occurred. He glanced round the room to ensure that he was still alone and slowly and with evil in his voice, he read out two of the names on the list.

Number four - Patrick Mahoney St Peters College, Loyola Hall, Burscough, Lancs PE13 6XU

Number five - Michael Flanders St Peters College, Loyola Hall, Burscough, Lancs PE13 6XU

If he kept this information to himself, no one would ever know.

And once more his role as Satan's adversary was about to take on a new form.

The sun had reached the meridian, and its scorching rays fell full on the glass panes, which seemed themselves sensible to the heat. He felt an indescribable sensation, somewhat akin to dread, that dread of the daylight which even in the desert makes us fear we are watched and observed. The feeling was so strong, that at the moment when Dermott was about to examine the rest of the list, he stopped, laid down the document, and walked toward the door and gazed round in every direction. There was no one else around and for some reason, this gave him re-assurance. He looked at the names once more. Was he awake, or was it but a dream? He leaned his head in his hands as if to prevent his senses from leaving him and then rushed madly around the room liked a man seized with frenzy. He was still unable to believe the evidence of his senses. Then he raised his eyes upwards and uttered a prayer intelligible to his God alone and then he yelled out loudly,

'By the sign of the devil, the God of vengeance, he yields to me his power to punish the wicked and I shall have my retribution!'

It was a night, at once joyous and terrible, such as this man of stupendous emotions had already experienced two or three times in his life.

Chapter Fifteen

The criminal stain that now seemed to be running in his blood, instead of being modified, was increased and rendered infinitely more dangerous by his extraordinary mental powers. He felt himself becoming the Napoleon of crime. He was becoming an organiser of evil. The genius, the philosopher and the abstract thinker all rolled into one mind. His brain was of the first order. He would sit motionless, like a spider in the centre of its web, but that web had a thousand radiations, and he knew well every quiver of each of them. He was a thinker, and he would stay in reflective mood for days on end, until his mind, stimulated by mental exaltation, reached a conclusion. It was then, and only then, that he would put his game plan in force. Eight days after receiving this list of names, he had formulated his course of action.

Dermott extracted an old green, battered book, from the shelves, in the backroom of the laboratory. From the layers of dust which had formed on the covers, it was apparent it had not been used for a long while. When Dermott shook off the dust the faded title could just about be read:

'The Companion of Forensic Science' by Dr H Loughton.

He turned to the index at the back and thumbed through the pages. He stopped at the letter P searching for the section on poisons and then turned to page 318. The items were listed in alphabetical order commencing with Accident. He moved on down the page and stopped at the section on ACONITE and commenced reading.

A drug derived from the common garden plant 'monkshood' (*aconitum anglicum*) though in some parts of the country it is called 'wolfsbane', 'leopard's bane', 'women's bane', and 'Devil's Helmet'; in Ireland, it is known as 'blue rocket'. He liked the reference to 'Devil's Helmet' thinking it a most appropriate title. He continued to read.

The active constituent of Aconite is an alkaloid called Aconitine, contained in a greater or lesser strength in the plant's foliage or root. In medicine, it was formerly administered in the form of tincture of aconite or as a liniment – usually for the relief of sciatica and rheumatism, where its heat-producing and mildly anaesthetic properties gave comfort. Aconitine fell into disfavour when it was found that even rubbing preparations on the skin produced symptoms of poisoning as by ingestion.

Until well into this century, it was the most virulent poison known, one-fiftieth of a grain proving fatal, while it is certain that one-tenth of a grain will always result in death. It is a white powder without any definite crystalline structure, hardly soluble in water, but dissolved by alcohol or weak acids. Dilutions of one-thousandth of a grain can be distinguished by the tingling sensation caused by the drug.

The symptoms of Aconitine poisoning are as follows: in a few minutes to an hour from the time of ingestion, the victim experiences a numbness and tingling sensation in the mouth and throat, which become parched. If a large quantity has been administered, this tingling becomes a severe burning extending down the throat and into the abdomen. The tingling rapidly extends to the hands and feet, and soon the whole surface of the body is affected. The skin of the extremities is cool and clammy to the touch, but at the same time, the victim complains that he feels as though his limbs have been flayed. There is a loss of power in the legs, and sight and hearing are considerably dulled, though usually the victim remains in full possession of his mental faculties until death ensues. Occasionally, muscular twitching is followed by convulsions. The pulse becomes weak and variable, the pupils of the eyes dilated, and the least exertion may bring on a fatal attack. Death usually results from failure of the respiratory organs. Aconitine paralyses all the organs in turn, and the fatal period can be from eight minutes to three or four hours.

The aconite poisons have been known throughout the world from the earliest of times, and the ancient Greeks called it the Queen of poisons and believed that it was created from the saliva of the mythical guardian dog of the underworld, Cerberus.

When Dermott had stopped reading, he felt a cold chill of disappointment. Although he had access to most of the poisons listed in the manual, the effects of administering this particular one, even in disguise, might leave him open to detection. He would have to think about this carefully.

He moved his eyes further down the page and stopped at another of the headings. This time it was ANTIMONY.

Antimony derives from the Greek *anthemonium*, 'flower like' from the shape of its crystals. Legend says that the poisonous properties of antimony were really discovered accidentally; under the original name of stibium, it was greatly used by Egyptian beauties to darken their eyelids and eyebrows. One of the princesses of the house of Urs-maat-Ra was apparently given to experimenting and selected one of her handmaids to try the effect of an oral dose of stibium. Needless to say, the girl did not survive the ordeal, and from that occasion, it is said, dates the use of antimony as a poison. The early Roman physicians fashioned little goblets from the silver-like metal, which were sold as emetic cups. The cups were filled with wine and left fermenting until such time as the bloated reveller could eat and drink no more, he then took a quaff from the cup, vomited violently, and was ready to continue feasting.

Antimony is found naturally in a metallic state, mixed with arsenic and silver, and for years the great difficulty in purifying the metal was getting rid of the arsenic.

The poisoner commonly obtains antimony in the form of a tartar emetic, or antimony tartrate, a white powder that leaves a strong taste of metal in the mouth. In doses of more than a grain at a time it is a strong emetic, and for that reason may not have a poisonous effect, being rejected before it has had time to exhibit its lethal properties. However, where a deadly dose has been administered, the patient exhibits all the symptoms of poisoning with a strong irritant. There is a sensation of burning in the throat, accompanied by difficulty in swallowing. This is followed by a violent pain in the stomach, incessant vomiting and diarrhoea, faintness and extreme depression provoked by a premonition of death. At the onset the pulse becomes accelerated, but then the blood pressure begins to fall and the pulse becomes slow and irregular. Sweating is profuse, and the skin cold and clammy to the touch. Now the extremities of the body and face exhibit a general blueness. Cramps in the calves of the legs are usually followed by spasmodic contractions, and vertigo. At this stage, the victim loses consciousness and death will follow from heart failure. In short, it is a most painful death and any chance of survival from poisoning is slim.

Dermott chuckled with maniacal laughter. 'That will be a fine penalty for Patrick and Michael together. In fact it will be too good a death for those two evil swines.'

He reasoned however, that antimony would be far more deadly if administered in repeated small quantities. He thought to himself, 'If

I administer it by regulating the doses, the victim can be killed without attracting unfavourable attention presenting symptoms of sickness, abdominal pain, loss of appetite and diarrhoea.' All these symptoms could surely be construed as compatible with AIDS destroying the immune system.

Looking further through the B index, he came upon Brucine. He remembered it well for it was the drug used by Madame de Villefort, in the Count of Monte Cristo. She tried to poison half her household. He also remembered that in days gone by, the brewers used to add this to their beer to enhance its bitterness. This practice was eventually outlawed for fear of poisoning the beer drinking population. This particular drug resembled strychnine in most characteristics, but carried only one-sixth of its strength. The problem was, he reasoned to himself; with, the accurate methods of analysing, which now existed, no person could administer a fatal dose of alkaloid to another without detection. No he would have to rule this one out of the plan.

He needed a poison that could be administered over a lengthy period so as to avoid detection, but nevertheless one, which would obtain the desired result in the long term.

He arrived at the C index and looked at the heading 'C*oniine*' : an oily liquid similar to nicotine extracted from the poison hemlock Conium maculatum, which is best known, as the judicial execution, of the Greek philosopher Socrates. The effects of the drug, so eloquently described by Plato, are not painful; the body becomes increasingly numb until the lungs fail or the heart is paralysed. There are no post-mortem signs save those found in cases of Asphyxia.

He reflected an instant and felt himself becoming agitated and his lips became white and his teeth clenched as he was consumed with apprehension.

'This will do nicely instead, compared with antimony, there is virtually no risk of detection,' he said as he renewed his oath of vengeance.

Chapter Sixteen

It was September and Britain was enjoying an Indian Summer.

Dermott was seated at his side table and working hard over a chemical investigation. A large curved retort was boiling furiously in the bluish flame of a Bunsen burner, and the distilled drops were condensing into a two-litre measure. He hardly glanced up as Bradstreet entered and Bradstreet seeing that his investigation must be of importance, seated himself in a chair and waited. He dipped into this bottle or that, drawing out a few drops of each with his glass pipette, and finally brought a test tube containing a solution over to the table. In his right hand he held a slip of litmus paper.

'You come at an important moment,' said Dermott. 'If this paper remains blue, all is well. If it turns red, the experiment fails.' He dipped it into the test tube and it flushed at once into a dull dirty crimson.

'Hum, I thought as much!' said Dermott. 'I will be with you in an instant Bradstreet.' He threw himself into the chair opposite and drew up his knees until his fingers clasped round his long, thin shins.

'A complicated experiment and I haven't found a solution. You have got something better in your hand, I fancy. You are the stormy petrel of medicine, Bradstreet. What is it?'

Bradstreet handed him the letter, which he read with the most concentrated attention.

'So the trials start next week. Have we got all the component compounds?'

'Yes, Dermott, I checked them personally only last week.'

'Well, I will commence making up the chemical elements tomorrow,' said Dermott struggling to contain his excitement.

The regulations for commencing the trials were strict, very strict. Not only was there to be two experts from the BMC present but the European acclaimed expert on AIDS was to preside over proceedings ensuring the compounds were accurate, pure and weighing correctly down to one-millionth of a gram. But Dermott had done his homework well, because for the three months previously, he had carried experiments on mice with almost prefect results. Now, however, his devious skills were about to enter the human arena with devastating effect.

The university employed the finest technology and equipment in the land and had become the renowned centre of excellence in the field of progressive medicine. All the acknowledged experts were present on the very first morning of the trials but only the elite allowed access to the main laboratory.

The morning started with the chemical compounds being cleaned, purified and crushed into a small white powder and then frozen at 1000 degrees minus centigrade. The powder was then shaped into white capsules of 100mg, 50mg, and 25mg per portion, and then allowed to dry in a special ventilator for three hours at 98 degrees Fahrenheit. At this stage, the capsules were packed by a mechanical packer so as to avoid human contamination and at the same time, keep them fresh for oral consumption. All this meant that Dermott would have to bide his time and wait for an opportune moment to exercise his plan. Personal packs of tablets were to be made up according to the individual needs of each patient. Initially, the patients were then personally to attend the university to receive their unique dosage that was to be administered by the BMC representative. Dermott's plan was to taint the compound with a millionth tincture of *coniine* and then hope that the ventilator would do its job in the drying process. It had worked upon the mice and the ingredients of the capsules had not altered one iota since that time. Patience of the utmost degree was required – patience and dedication, and with regard to the former, the patience of Job would be required. The months ticked slowly by and the cold March winds blasted the country from the East when Dermott felt relaxed enough to act as Satan's accomplice. The patients had remained stable throughout the first six months and the security around the process laboratory whilst still strict was nevertheless now strict, in a *relaxed sort of way*. Now there was only one representative from the BMC and the acclaimed European expert had travelled back from whence he came.

This left Dermott, Bradstreet and the representative, to preside over proceedings and Dermott had bided his time for long enough.

It was a warm April morning and Dermott and Bradstreet were checking the names of the list of patients when the internal telephone rang.

'Main lab, Bradstreet speaking. Oh I see, what time will he arrive then, yes, ok, no problem.' Bradstreet finished on the telephone and turned to Dermott.

'Bentley is going to be late, he suggests we may as well start the preparations. Nothing has been flawed to date. Says he should arrive around 11.30am.' Dermott involuntarily raised his eyes to heaven and whispered something to himself. Now he knew his time had come. He would not get another opportunity such as this. He looked at his watch. 'Soon be coffee time,' he muttered to his colleague.

'Yes, let's have it now,' returned Bradstreet. '48 for you and I think I will have a Mochachino. Back in a couple of minutes,' and with that, he disappeared downstairs. Dermott could not believe his luck and he was unsure just how much time he had. He moved quickly, trying to steady his hand as he extracted the white powder from its receptacle. Now he was nervous of Bradstreet returning. He guessed that he had about four minutes to spare. The vending machine was two floors below and there was sometimes a queue. He extracted the coniine fluid with the delicate laboratory instruments giving a reading of one-millionth of a measure. He was becoming increasingly nervous that Bradstreet was about to return. He put down his instruments and walked to the door to ensure he was not being watched. My God he thought; How strong is this feeling of guilt and fear. He felt unseen eyes watching his every move, but there was no one there save himself. He watched with meticulous care as the minute amount of deadly fluid merged with the white powder, undetectable to the naked eye. Still no sign of Bradstreet, he was now beginning to sweat profusely. What was keeping him? He took the white powder and gently placed it in the special freezer, still anticipating his colleague to re-appear. No sign of him. He began to repeat the process and now he had two sets of compound in the special freezer. He checked his watch. Nine minutes had elapsed. No Bradstreet. Repeating the process a third time, he was about to seal up the deadly death fluid when he heard Bradstreet's footsteps in the passageway.

'Sorry, Dermott, the coffee machine had run out. Had to wait until it was refilled.'

'No problem, I have started proceedings.' He half expected Bradstreet to launch into the regulations about having two people present during the preparation period. But Bradstreet trusted his colleague implicitly and nothing was said. Now Dermott diligently moved away the receptacle containing the death poison, trying to ensure he had aroused no suspicion. It was much later in the day when two workmates ensured the first batch of antidotes were extracted from the drying ventilator, and the three tablets 100mg 50mg and 25mg were transferred into their seal tight packaging, ready for final examination and transportation. Dermott was now the *'keeper of the lists'* and was about to sign the final part of the death warrant for one of his main enemies.

The computer flickered into life and the names of the patients spewed forth in the form of a sticky label. Dermott ensured that batch number five was allocated specifically to a certain Patrick Mahoney resident at St Peter's College, Burscough. If successful in his goal, Peter Flanders would also receive a deadly cocktail in the months to come.

Chapter Seventeen

It was a blazing hot day in May as Dermott strolled up the steps of the GRO office in Dublin. Dermott walked up to the reception desk to ask for assistance.
'Can I help you?' A tall man with horn-rimmed spectacles had asked the question.
'Yes, can you show me where I can find the birth records?'
'Any particular year?'
'Yes, 1968 or thereabouts.'
The tall man led Dermott off down a side aisle where row upon row of volumes were stacked neatly upon the shelves. He found the third quarter for 1968 and commenced looking for the section containing Murray. Sure enough the volume yielded the information he was looking for, only this time he was about to obtain his own private copy. This copy he was going to show his beloved Teresa in three days time when he had arranged to meet up with her. This meeting he had pre-arranged with Teresa and deliberately concealed from Shelagh. In fact, he had informed Shelagh he was undertaking a walking expedition in the South-West area, of Ireland. He had told her he was climbing Brandon Mountain and Macgillycuddy's Reeks near County Kerry. And that was a long way from Dublin. By the time he had accomplished this, his short break would be over and there would be no time to visit the fair city. But he had become hardened and telling untruths had become second nature to him.

Unsure of just how he was going to broach the subject with Teresa, he practised his script and practised daily until he no longer needed to refer to his mental notes. He learnt to say the words as naturally as he could, because he didn't wish to cause her any anguish. But just how did one tell ones cousin, that you were not cousins at all, but in fact Brother and Sister!

Dermott was pacing up and down the library steps unable to contain his excitement when he saw Teresa walking towards him through the thronging crowd.

'Teresa, over here,' and as he uttered the words, he felt his heart dilate and throb. He opened his arms and Teresa uttering a cry sprang into them. They embraced and Dermott expecting a passionate embrace, could not contain himself, but as Teresa imprinted her kiss on his cheek, he felt that it was with no greater warmth, than she would have respectfully bestowed on the hand of some marble statue of a saint. He suddenly realised that *his* first intention had been to re-kindle the passions, that had first rose to the surface on that summer day, but he had to check himself as he remembered, that this was his sister.

'Is everything all right?'

'Yes, of course it is. We have so much to talk about and I have so much to tell you.' For some reason this last comment made him feel uneasy.

The first hours passed very quickly as the small talk and reminiscences took a hold. He wondered how he could explain to Teresa what he had discovered without causing any distress.

'You know none of us back home know anything about your life here in Ireland. All Shelagh has ever told us is that you live with aunt Josie, mother's younger sister and your stepfather Fergal.'

'Oh, Dermott, that's not very exciting, life at home is as dull as ditch-water. Tell me, Dermott, do you have a girlfriend back home?' He blushed as he remembered once more the day of forbidden passion.

'Er, well not at present but I am working on it.' He wondered why she had asked the question in such a forthright manner.

'Dermott, I have something to tell you and I hope you will be pleased for me.' He was about to answer but she interjected once more.

'Dermott, I have met a wonderful man and we are going to be married.' Dermott felt an indescribable pang in his heart and his jaw dropped in a crestfallen manner. He struggled for something to say and then he mumbled with as much feeling as he could muster.

'Married, but I thought we could spend some time together,' and as the words came out he then knew instantly, that he would never be able to relate his findings to her. And as he felt his lustful desires take over his whole being once more, he thought of the 'old tempter' who had now changed the course of his life so dramatically.

'Well, we can,' and she clasped one of his hands in her own squeezing it affectionately. This gesture confused him, but she then added, 'I would like you both to meet and I hope you like each other.'

One again Dermott was stupefied. As a brother and sister, there could be no hope for them both as a couple. But now other emotions were rising to the surface and about to take control of his very being if he let them. To possess Teresa albeit fleetingly, would mean happiness so infinite, so ecstatic, so complete and too divine for this world. Lust on its own could be a poison arrow. But lust combined with jealously was a deadly concoction in whatever form it was displayed. He was unable to have Teresa to himself but neither did he want a rival to take her. The blood of Satan was once more flowing through his veins. He now believed he had inherited the evil genes, the genes that would force him to see his task through to the end.

His countenance changed and he forced himself to be relaxed and frivolous and Teresa did not notice the envy that was making him fraught with tension, for he was now the wolf in sheep's clothing.

'So I will meet you at O' Flannagan's at 7pm. Will it be all right if I bring Eammon this evening?' He was brutalised with envy but overshadowed with desire and he forced a natural reply.

'Yes, I will look forward to it,' and they parted with Dermott cursing his bad luck.

Dermott stared with disbelief as he gazed upon his rival Eammon. Instead of the young handsome athletic man he expected was a rather thin, almost frail human being, with craggy features and an almost receding hairline. Coupled with this fact, he also looked about ten years older than Teresa, almost like a sugar daddy. He was flash and adorned with a gold ring and gold expensive wrist-watch.

Dermott extended a fake cordial handshake.

'Pleased to meet you.'

'Likewise,' replied Eammon. 'Teresa has told me all about you.' Dermott felt uncomfortable with this remark, as if another blow had been struck against his weakening armour.

'A pioneer in medicine.'

'Oh, I wouldn't go as far as that, she is just being kind.'

'How about you?' Eammon looked pleased, as if he had been waiting for this opportunity to expand on himself. I made my money in commodities trading about ten years ago and now I run E D Enterprises, my own company with a £50million turnover.' Dermott thought to himself 'So he is a sugar daddy after all. No wonder she is attracted to him, just think of the security he can offer a young woman like that.'

Dermott's awful evening continued and his misery was complete when Teresa invited him to the wedding which was booked for the following March.

Towards the end of the evening Eammon suddenly started.

'You must excuse me for leaving so early, but I have to be at the airport for 6am tomorrow. I have a business trip to Amsterdam. I have arranged a taxi for Teresa. The driver can drop you off as well. Nice meeting you,' and with that Teresa rose from the table and walked with Eammon to the door, exchanged some words and a fleeting embrace and returned quickly to Dermott.

Now his passion and jealousy were almost at boiling point and he struggled for something to say. His rival had now become one of his enemies, not because he had injured Dermott in any way, but because of what he represented. A slimy specimen who had prostituted Teresa's love. Did he think he could buy her with lavish gifts? Security was on display not love. Teresa suddenly became more relaxed as she poured the last of the wine taking both her own portion and that of Demott's after he had declined.

'You probably feel he is too old and not really suitable for me, but he takes care of me.' Now the forces of good and evil were pounding at each other. Here was an opportunity to change the subject and tell her of his findings, but as he gazed upon her beauty, his intention melted away, and he moved on to Josie and Fergal.

'You never ever talk about your mum or stepfather Fergal. What is he like?'

'What is there to say. Mum treats me as if I am the apple of her eye and Fergal spoils me too. Dermott what do you really feel about Eammon?'

'Well are you absolutely sure about being married? Whilst Eammon treats you like an angel remember, he is a lot older than you. Have you tried to think ahead say in 20 years time?'

'Well, I occasionally have my doubts but I can only share that fact with you. Do you know what I mean, Dermott?' And as she said the words she gazed lovingly into Dermott's eyes and extended both her arms towards him.

'Do you ever think about those days gone by when I used to visit you and the girls?'

'All the time,' replied Dermott. 'Do you remember the day in the rain?' asked Dermott.

'How could I ever forget it? You know, Dermott, if only we were not cousins,' continued she, with a feeling of profound melancholy.

Dermott felt his brow, darken more and more, and he became filled again with apprehension. This was his golden opportunity and yet he could not force himself to speak. It was as though an invisible force had stripped him of his vocal chords. He knew it was the force of the devil once more rising up inside him. He changed his tack.

'Well, we are not that closely related. It is not as if we are brother and sister.'

'No but we are too close aren't we?'

'Depends in whose eyes we are looking through.'

'Here comes the taxi, fancy a night-cap at my hotel, before you go home?'

'Yes ok, just the one, mind you.'

By the time the third drink had been consumed Teresa's coquettishness had once more risen to the surface.

'You know, Dermott, the comparison I draw between you and other men will forever be one of my greatest tortures,' and as she spoke she shifted her body round and looked directly into his eyes.

'Why don't we have a coffee in my room before we both become terribly drunk,' and with that they ambled slowly across the floor towards the lift. It was six in the morning when the two confused beings arose to the world and Dermott gave thanks to his new found God, for allowing him the opportunity to exercise his passionate indulgence.

Chapter Eighteen

It was a Thursday, the day before Dermott was returning to the mainland. The two of them had arranged to meet in the evening for one last time. Both were tortured by passionate flashbacks and a tinge of guilt, or in Teresa's case, with a lot of guilt. But Dermott had always been her 'knight in shining armour' and he exercised a great influence over her. A cab was splashing its way though the city centre with a single occupant. It was the young and beautiful Teresa who looked radiant from the exterior, but who trembled on the inside with a mixture of excitement and fear. Amid the droning of the wind and heavy rain came the sharp grind of the wheel as it rasped against the curb. Teresa hurriedly stepped out and rushed into the hotel almost forgetting to pay for her fare. She paid the cabby and walked quickly up the hotel steps. She greeted Dermott in a state of almost uncontrollable agitation.

'Dermott, my conscience has been troubling me since the other evening. I feel I have let Eammon down.' Dermott shrugged his shoulders in ungracious acquiescence.

'Listen, it just happened,' and with this comment he pulled her more closely. Once more she got a whiff of his scent. A combination, of his own bodily smell, and the faintest fragrance of 'aftershave'.

'We must not let this happen again,' and as she spoke the tears chased each other down her beautiful cheeks, the unhappy woman's heart was breaking, as memory recalled the recent changeful events of her life.

'Dermott, I am no longer a reasoning woman.'

'Teresa, we are all free agents.'

'That is not so, because I have free will, but I have not got the power to render that will efficacious. This is all too much! Dermott, we are caught between two stools.' He dropped his head and shrank from the vehemence of her grief.

'Will you not say you will see me again?'

'Dermott, after this evening we cannot meet again until the wedding.' Teresa let her head and arms fall; her legs bent under her, and she almost sank to her knees, until Dermott restrained her. He pulled her close into his chest and gently placed a kiss behind her ear. She weakened once more and responded with a warm passionate kiss herself as if trying to convey a message without speaking. She remembered thinking, 'Forgive me Eammon, forgive for my sake because I love this man.'

They disappeared once more upstairs and once more enacted the scene of two lovers who had not a thought in the world, save for their own mutual satisfaction.

Teresa opened her eyes to see the morning sun peeping through the gap in curtains. The passionate couple lay side by side like two spoons. She felt warm and happy for a few brief seconds and then reality set in. This happiness was only fleeting because now she had to face another day in the real world. She could feel an abyss being created between her real world and her imaginary world with Dermott. Betrayal now oozed from her every tissue. She had let down her betrothed once again. She tried to convince herself that what is not known cannot hurt you. She remembered the vast amounts of alcohol they had consumed before their bout of passion and then how they had both fallen into a drunken stupor. And then a sobering thought brought her back to reality with a severe jolt. 'My God we threw caution to the wind, I hope I haven't been caught out.' Dermott was beginning to return to consciousness.

'Good morning, my little treasure.'

'Dermott, I have just had a thought.'

'What's that, my love?'

'Dermott, we were not very careful. I hope everything will be ok. If I find myself pregnant that will be the end of everything in my life.'

Teresa's remark caused him to sit bolt upright in the bed. Her comment sent a spasm of panic through his whole frame. He was trembling inside and a fear so strong, so rigid, was threatening to engulf him.

'What are the chances of that happening?'

'Well, it wasn't the best time for us to have done what we did, that is for sure.' On hearing this, he descended into a deep silence.

'Dermott, tell me what you are thinking, I hate it when you go so quiet.'

'I was just thinking about the problems it would cause if you do become pregnant.'

'Dermott, we shouldn't have been so weak. I feel bad about

Eammon again.' But once more he was engrossed with his own thoughts, thoughts he wished to share with Teresa, but couldn't. To have made love to someone else's betrothed was bad enough, but to make ones sister pregnant, was the cardinal sin of all mankind.

'If Shelagh could see us now she would kill us.'

'So, too, would Josie and Fergal. Even though he is not my real father, he treats me as if I am his own daughter.' He let her remark die away for a few seconds and then he replied.

'Teresa, my love, where is your real father?'

'Dermott, I don't know, he left us before I was born. Josie never refers to him, not even by name. She says he was from bad stock, a very bad type.'

'Have you never wanted to trace him?'

'No, I don't wish to know him if he that sort and what's more, Fergal is a lovely stepfather.'

'Haven't Josie and Fergal ever wanted children of their own?'

'Well, unfortunately, mum says she cannot have any more, something wrong inside, you know, a woman's problem. It would have been nice to have had a brother though.' He made a move to the bathroom to disguise the fact that his cheeks were colouring up. These few words that Teresa had uttered stayed in his mind. He was from bad stock. That tied in with the description that Dermott now had of his self. Like father, like son he thought. Unexplained questions began rising to the surface. Why was Josie the guardian of Teresa? And just where was Dermott's father, the father of them all?

May moved into June and the telephone rang once more in Dermott's office. It was an agitated Teresa.

'Dermott, we have got to meet something terrible has happened!'

'Teresa, my love, what's the problem?'

'Dermott, I am pregnant!'

'Oh my God,' and his voice trailed off as if not knowing what to say next. Suddenly his agitation became extreme and large drops of perspiration rolled from his heated brows.

'You sure?'

'Of course I am sure and it's our child, it's definitely not Eammon's.' Terror began to form in every fibre and tissue of his body and he could no longer think clearly. Bradstreet entered the room and he appeared not to perceive him. 'Is everything ok, you look as white as a sheet?' He tried to disguise his fear and replied in a stuttering manner.

'Oh yes, fine,' and then he continued his conversation with Teresa.

'Dermott, you will have to come over to discuss this. When can you come?'

His agitation increased and he muttered a few words.

'Next weekend, I will fly to Dublin, first flight out. Meet me at the hotel about 10.30am, bye for now.' He tried to hide his nervous state from his colleague and wandered off to the coffee machine trying to appear calm. All his emotion now burst forth and he walked out of the building and began asking his master why he had been deserted in this hour of need. Now he was troubled. His mentor seemed to have deserted him and his role as the mighty avenger appeared to have been reversed with one foul stroke and the implications of Teresa carrying their child were too frightening to think about.

Dermott took a sip of his wine and looked lovingly into Teresa's eyes. She spoke first.

'Dermott, what are we going to do?'

'Does Eammon know?'

'No, only you and I.'

'Are you still going ahead with the wedding?'

'Dermott, I have to.'

'You don't have to do anything.'

'I can't cancel the wedding, it would break his heart.'

'That would make three broken hearts then.'

'I could have this baby and not tell Eammon. The implications of telling him are too horrendous to contemplate. The third option is out of the question. Terminating a life is just a no go area.'

'It would solve all the problems.'

'Dermott, is that what you want, to destroy this life we have made? Even though we are cousins we cannot murder this child.' Yet another opportunity had arisen for Dermott to come clean, but he was already in too deep and he shirked his responsibility once more.

'Dermott, I have thought about this for days. The only sensible option is for the wedding to go ahead and let Eammon think he is the father.' Now she looked towards Dermott for some sort of reassurance. But he had already decided in his heart that he would accede to her wishes, whatever they may be, because he was made that way and because he loved her. Her wishes were his wishes. Whilst he couldn't say he had been let off the hook he had certainly been granted a stay of execution.

Chapter Nineteen

Patrick Mahoney placed the capsule on his tongue took a large swig of water and washed down his antidote. He had been feeling strong for about three and a half months now. At first, he thought it had just been the placebo effect but now he was convinced the prescription was working to his good effect. He had been taking the miraculous drug regularly and his strength seemed to be gaining day by day. His nervous system was an exceptionally sensitive one, able to detect the slightest physical malfunction of any part of his body. If his progress continued at this rate, he would be able to go walking in the country in the near future. His improvement had proved exemplary. By the time he was ready for his next dose, it was suggested that he give himself a complete change of scene and air. Thus he found himself in a small cottage, rented by the church, at the further extremity of a Devon bay. It was a singular spot and one peculiarly suited to the grim state of mind Patrick Mahoney was in. From the windows of the little whitewashed cottage, which stood high on a grassy headland, he could look down on the sinister semicircle of the bay, with its fringe of black cliffs and rocks on which innumerable seamen had met their end. With a northerly breeze it lay placid and sheltered, inviting storm tossed craft to tack into it for rest and protection. Right from this moment he felt rested and protected but he wondered just when he would meet his own end. Had the grim reaper postponed the death call for a while to come?

On the land side, the surroundings were as sombre as on the sea. It was a country of rolling moors, lonely and dun coloured, with an occasional church tower to mark the site of some old-world village. In every direction upon the moors there were traces of some vanished race, which had passed away, and left strange monuments of stone, irregular mounds which contained the burned ashes of the dead, and curious earthworks which hinted at prehistoric strife. The glamour and mystery of the place, with its sinister atmosphere of forgotten nations, began to appeal to Patrick Mahoney and he spent much of his time in long walks and solitary meditations upon the moor. He had received a consignment of books upon philosophy and was settling down to develop a thesis when he found himself suddenly, even in his land of dreams, plunged into a spasm of despair. His simple life and peaceful, healthy routine was violently interrupted by bouts of fear. Fears of ill health and fears of being struck down with the dreadful disease that was inside his immune system, were followed by an overriding fear of imminent death. He asked himself time and time again, 'Why should I not live for many years to come. The medication seems to be working. This must all be in the mind.'

One afternoon he started off sturdily up the cliffs surrounding the bay. About half way up the towering cliff his progress became ludicrously slow. Every foot he gained in height was an effort. His legs became so weak that he was now forced to rest every five or six steps, and soon the fatigue made him forget everything except that he was Patrick Mahoney and he was suffering from AIDS. At last at the base of the final rock outcrop, he could go no further. Various thoughts flashed through his mind. Had he ever been so tired before? Would he be less tired another day? He had reached his limit. Soon he turned back and staggered down to the starting point. There he lay in the sun and rested. After 15 or 20 minutes of complete rest he counted his pulse. It was 155. Suddenly, he tried to look years ahead into the future so as to cement firmly in his mind recollections of the past. Now he felt all his previous life had reached a climax in the last 20 minutes. This was no struggle against nature, he was now battling with his body. His musings were interrupted by a shout from below.

Another walker was calling, but it was not to him, it was to her dog that bounded up the steep path oblivious to the poor man resting at the bottom. Oh what he would give to be able to turn back the clock. Then as quickly as it had arrived, the attack disappeared. 'Perhaps this was just a panic attack brought on by my subconscious,' he thought. He walked slowly back to the cottage and drowsed off into a dreamless sleep.

Dermott had been scrutinising the medical records of the AIDS volunteers with the utmost diligence. All patients had been responding well to the new drugs – very well. Now it was time to step up the game. Bradstreet was in a meeting all morning. This time, he prepared four more capsules and laced them with the deadly potion once more ensuring they were destined for Patrick Mahoney.

Over the coming months the deadly cocktails would eventually reach their destined home and once more Satan would have had his retribution. Dermott began to regularly feel the enormous 'high' which was a result of the power he yielded over his enemies. If crime did not actually pay, joining forces with the devil had offered nothing but pluses. Whilst he did not 'pray' to his new master he would often whisper incantations to himself, 'Help me oh satanic one' was a regular theme.

This new found power was becoming an addiction. The practice was easier to attain than to get rid of and he was becoming a slave to it all, an object of mingled horror and pity. But sadly as he was not looking from the outside in, he could not see the pathological and morbid specimen he was becoming.

Chapter Twenty

Yet another month went by of Patrick Mahoney's treatment. His iron constitution had shown little signs of giving way, save for the one occasion, a couple of months previously. But now he was noticing he needed to rest at the least exertion and his extremities occasionally felt as though they were numb. 'Perhaps it is the drugs that don't agree with me,' he said out-loud. The thought was correct, just the diagnosis was wrong. He had been engaged in a long walk and solitary meditation on the moors and was setting off back toward home, when suddenly he began gasping and then coughing. He staggered towards a rocky outcrop trying to draw air into his lungs. He seemed to be beside himself with excitement. His two eyes shone like stars and the features were working convulsively. He was becoming blue-lipped and insensible, with a swollen congested face and protruding eyes. Now his whole body seemed numb and so distorted were his features that he would have failed to recognise himself had he been carrying a mirror with him. He was striving for oxygen and yet he was hardly at any real height above sea level. He had heard of pulmonary oedema but remembered that was an ailment, that mountaineer's contract. However, he was still living and after resting a while, the strange symptoms passed off. He made his way with great difficulty back to his cottage of refuge.

The telephone rang once more in Dermott's office.

'Chief M O speaking. Dermott, one of the trialists has had some sort of relapse. We need a meeting ASAP. The others are all ok.'

'Oh, that is a disappointment, which one is it?'

'Someone named Patrick Mahoney. How about next Thursday?'

'Yes, that's fine. I will bring all the ancillary file notes.' Any one gazing upon Dermott at this precise moment would have noted his complexion turning very pale, for now the game was afoot for real. But if they had looked that bit closer, they could have also seen an unappeasable hatred in his eyes. The devil was once more on the warpath.

The stout florid faced Chairman with red hair brought the meeting to a close.

'So, that is it settled then, gentlemen. We will increase the strength of the treatment for two months, but check this Patrick Mahoney's respiratory track first. Just to ensure he is not allergic to any of the components. Any further comments.' Dermott put on his look of composure.

'It may just be that the virus has weakened his immune system that little bit more than the rest of the patients. We always knew this would be the weak link in our prognosis.'

'Yes, and we informed them all their could be no guarantees. Right everyone, we will meet again in six weeks time.' Now the executioner knew that one more dose would achieve the desired effect and he summoned all his sufferings to the aid of his goal.

The scorching rays of the midday sun fell full upon the rocks when Patrick was about to commence his walk. He could hear grasshoppers in the bushes and he disturbed a butterfly resting among the foliage with its back glittering with hue of the emerald. In 15 minutes he saw himself on the highest point of the imminent coastline, a statue on a vast pedestal of granite, no other human in sight, whilst the blue ocean beat against the base of the rocks below, and covered them with a fringe of foam. Then he descended with a cautious and slow step gazing around in every direction. He remained motionless and thoughtful.

'Come,' said he to himself.

'I must not be downcast again I have suffered no further attacks for a while,' and once more he set off towards his cottage. About three in the afternoon, he was in high spirits and a feeling of well being took hold of his countenance. A brisk walk found him at the water's edge and he began to walk towards the caves, which were now accessible, as the tide was on the turn.

This was new territory for him as he entered the first cavern. Instead of the darkness, and the thick mephitic atmosphere he had expected to find, he saw a dim bluish light, which, as well as the air, entered not merely by the aperture he had just come through, but by the interstices and crevices of the rock which were just visible from without, and through which, he could distinguish the blue sky and the waving branches of the creepers, that grew from the rocks.

He stood a few minutes in the cavern, the atmosphere of which was rather warm than damp. His sharp eye could pierce the remotest angles of the cave and he saw in the farthest angle of the second opening a second grotto, which penetrated deeper into the gloom.

He could see that to investigate still further he had to cross a channel which fell away to an unseen depth and, which had been covered by a foaming torrent, some hours previously. Summoning the courage to jump the precipice, which was too wide to step across, he made a giant leap and in trying to protect himself from fall into the abyss, fell rather than landed, against the sharp rocks that cut into his flesh. He was severely winded and his right arm used to cushion the blow was bruised badly. He felt a tingling sensation in his arm and was suddenly gripped by a paroxysm of fear. His strength seemed to be ebbing away and now he could feel his arm becoming numb. My God he thought; must have been a severe jolt to cause this.

Now he was unsure if he could make the manoeuvre back across the gap if he had too. Looking for an alternative route out through the numerous grottoes and caves in the base of the cliff, he soon discovered they were too steep, too deep, or too narrow. Some of them were quite claustrophobic. He would have to return! 'But before I return, I must have a rest,' he whispered to himself. He lay down and now he noticed his left arm was also numb. He tried to remain calm because he could still feel no pain save for his bruised arm and even that seemed to be wearing off. Must be the endorphins; he thought. Lifting his body once, more he tried to gauge the effort required to jump back across the deep fissure. Now his legs felt numb and he sat crumpled in a sorry heap. He felt a desire for a long sleep that would wash away his fears and thoughts of the possible peril ahead and what appeared to be the hopelessness of his plight. No, he must not yield to this temptation, he might not wake up again. It felt that his feet were becoming laden and he took off his left shoe and sock to examine his foot. The sight of his foot was a hammer blow to the heart. It appeared swollen and there was no feeling at all. He did the same with his right shoe and sock. A wave of despair rode over him. He sat aghast, staring at his ruined feet he had trusted to jump the yawning gap. One thing was now absolutely certain, he could not now return the way he had come!

The shock once more told heavily on him. He found the sun's light falling on his face and he found it refreshing. Suddenly, he was seized with the idea that the solar energy would benefit his body. He pulled off his shirt and lay down to expose his body to the light streaming from the sky. Bathing in the glorious kiss of the sun, he felt an instant feeling of well being tingling through his body. He felt exhilarated, a sensation that flooded his senses. The sunlight's energy seemed to glow under his skin, to stimulate restorative processes, that eased the deep anxiety roused by the state of his feet and this made him feel stronger and more confident. He lay in this light until he felt a slight chill and he knew it was time for him to make a move. But to where? Now he was aware of a dreadful fact that had escaped his notice for a while. The tide was now washing into the mouth of his cavern. His nerves were frayed but he could feel no pain. His mind became hungry for sound, the sound of another human being. He could just make out the fine lines of a vessel heading out of the bay and in his panic began screaming at the unknown craft and her crew. He soon realised the sheer folly of it all because the sound of the waves crashing in around him drowned every audible noise for miles around. 'Perhaps someone on the cliffs will hear me,' he thought. But that also was to no avail.

Now the water began to rise. At best it was about three feet below him, but starting to rise and it would soon threaten to engulf him in a watery grave. He looked around despairingly, his only exit was the way he had come, across the gap. His strength was failing him but he still felt no pain but now his whole body felt cumbersome. He couldn't feel his feet anymore and the feeling had drained from his fingers and hands. What was happening? Half an hour passed away and then another 15 minutes and the tide rose steadily and the spray was beginning to splash him. He tried to wipe away the splashes on his hands and face, but all feeling had long since left his extremities. His arms and legs were now totally leaden as if the dentist had injected the numbing agent directly into his arteries. His movement became laboured and the fear that had overcome him was strangling him both physically and emotionally. 'I am going to have to jump,' he thought. But his mind was telling him one thing and his body doing another. Now the sea was lapping his ankles and he felt a sense of desolation.

'I am going to have to jump somehow,' he screamed out loud, but there was no one to hear him. Now his *whole* body felt heavy and he could feel no sensation in any of his limbs. 'My body is going numb,' he thought.

Now his rhythmic breathing was becoming laboured and he found he was hyperventilating. And now his heart felt as if it was tightening. 'Oh my God, please help me. What is happening to me?

Please don't let me die!' He found himself whispering the words rather than speaking them, because the effort was becoming too much for him. The noise of the incoming sea was becoming frightening, as he knew instinctively that this would be his watery grave if he did not jump. 'Jump, jump!' he could hear himself shouting or was it his imagination. All his senses appeared to be blurred as if his whole body was solidifying. His lungs were failing and filling with fluid and despite the lack of oxygen, he made final superhuman effort, brought on by fear of death and he tried to leap back across the chasm. 'Jump, Patrick, jump!'

He hit the rock almost perfectly, he had gauged his jump to perfection but his arms were totally devoid of any sensation and he had no grip. His hands tried to get some purchase on the protruding rocks but it was to no avail and he slid into the foaming torrent, his lungs drowned by a combination of the internal fluid and deadly seawater. His lungs had failed and his heart had been paralysed and the deadly *Coniine* had made its mark.

Three days later the remains of a carcass, with what looked like glazed sunken eyes and dreadful livid cheeks, was washed up on the shoreline, it was the remains of Patrick Mahoney.

When Dermott heard the bulletin on the national news, he felt giddy as if he were being suffocated. His normally composed nature was seized by a fit of trembling and fear. Fear of being discovered, as the culprit, the murderer. But there was no need for him to fear because he didn't need an alibi. The AIDS virus was the killer, he was merely an accomplice, and no one else could ever possibly know that fact.

He notified the authorities immediately before the coroner could compile a report, under the disguised pretext of wanting to assist. His brief synopsis was along the following lines:

I note from the national news, that a certain Patrick Mahoney was drowned at sea several days ago and I write to inform you that he was one of several volunteer patients, being treated with a new drug to combat the effects of the deadly AIDS virus. Should you require any further information please contact the British Medical Council at the address above quoting reference bc/serum 518. The coroner did indeed request further information, in fact he requested the full file of medical evidence for the said Patrick Mahoney.

A shadow passed over Dermott's brow and he began to feel

uneasy but the request had to be complied with, and the administration assistant sent the information forthwith. But the culprit need not have worried because several days later, the coroner's verdict was announced and a copy sent to the administrator at Dermott's office.

It informed the authorities that Patrick Mahoney had died from asphyxia and there was no sign of any other abnormalities unless one considered the side effects of the AIDS virus. In fact, the only sign of anything remotely abnormal was 'The Sign of the Devil' and that was hidden from the world at large, by its representative;

Dermott Murray!

Chapter Twenty One

Eammon was secretly in awe of Teresa and he seldom interfered with her and usually let her have her own way whatever the circumstances. But for three days now, she had been sinking. He was horrified for he had not noticed just how ill she looked. Her gaunt wasted face sent a chill to his heart. Her eyes had the brightness of fever and there was a hectic flush on either cheek.

'Teresa, I am sending for the doctor this very hour. I know you don't like a fuss but you need to be seen. There are two of you now and I don't wish either of you to be ill. This child of ours is taxing your strength.'

'Send for Dr White then, Eammon.'

She was indeed a deplorable sight. In the dim light of a foggy November day, the sick room was a gloomy spot, but Teresa's condition rendered it even more a dismal spectacle. Dr White looked at the sickly woman lying on the bed. She lay listlessly unable to move. All his professional instincts were aroused. He turned to Eammon and whispered under his breath.

'Well, Eammon, she seems to be in a pretty bad way. I am afraid I need to refer her to a specialist.'

'What do you think is a matter with her?'

'Well, just to be on the safe side, I need to get her referred. She has some sort of fever. Three days of absolute fast has not improved her condition, but she seems to be holding her own.' Five days later the consultant requested a meeting with Eammon alone.

'Eammon, she is stable but not actually improving. We need to carry out more tests.'

'That is fine doctor but what exactly is the problem?'

'Well, to date we have isolated it down to a rare blood disease. But we need to carry out more blood tests. In actual fact, we need to take a blood sample from yourself to ensure there is no complication with the baby.'

'You are sure they will both be all right?'

'Well, let's hope so, no cause for alarm just yet.'

Back on the mainland, Dermott was becoming uneasy. The

implications of his actions were starting to play on his mind. Was he somehow responsible for her illness? No, he couldn't be, but he was responsible for her pregnancy. Gloomy spectres began to haunt his mind. What if the baby turned out to be mad or had some other genetic or physical defect? How did he stand in the eyes of the law if the world found out his dark secret? What would happen if Eammon found out? He cursed his weakness and thought about the trap he had fallen into. All his desires and wishes had been falling into place, according to his master plan. But now, suddenly a major blip had occurred. He reminded himself that he had been born an adversary of the devil and that he was a disciple of Satan and therefore not to expect an easy ride. Those who follow the chaotic path must live by chaotic rules. He once again recalled his sufferings to give himself moral support and at the same time he requested that he be kept free from harm and successful in all his goals.

The doctor looked across at Eammon and tried to recover his ruffled composure. Eammon could tell from his body language that all was not well and prepared himself for the worse.

'Doctor, I fear you have some bad news for me, judging by the look on your face.'

The doctor looked grave.

'Eammon, I don't know how to put this, it is rather delicate.'

'It is the baby, I am sure.'

'Well actually it is not the baby.'

'Oh my God, it's Teresa, I knew it. What is the problem?'

'Eammon, it's not either of them.'

'Well, what is the problem?'

The doctor tried to strangle his emotion.

'Eammon, you remember we took some blood tests from all three of you; an abnormality has appeared in your sample.'

'In mine. That can't be correct, I am as fit as a fiddle.'

'Well, yes you are alright at present but we need to do some further checks with fresh samples.'

'What appears to be the problem? Do I smoke too much?'

The doctor paused before answering.

'Eammon, it is not as simple as that. We just want to do another analysis to eradicate the possibility of leukaemia.'

Eammon's jaw fell.

'Leukaemia, I have leukaemia?'

'We are not 100 percent sure. We just need to carry out a few more checks.' Eammon's demeanour altered. He immediately became ashened faced and started to tremble.

'How long will these tests take?'

'Well, if we start immediately, about three days.'

His thoughts suddenly transferred to Teresa.

'What about Teresa and the baby?'

This was becoming more difficult for the doctor than he could have possibly imagined.

'She is starting to recover and both her and your child should be alright.'

Eammon paused. 'Let's get this sorted then.'

'Eammon, call back here on Thursday, we will have the results ready,' and with that, the doctor brought the meeting to an end. Eammon, dazed from the revelation by the doctor, went about his business with perfunctory attention for the next three days. At last at the end of this period, he walked up the hospital steps in a daze. This time the doctor looked even paler than before, and as Eammon entered the room, he had to hold on tightly to the chair which was offered to him, as there were not one, but three people present. This did not look promising.

'Eammon, meetings such as this are always difficult,' began the plump man who was obviously the senior consultant.

'What exactly is the problem?'

'Eammon, the tests we carried out have now been analysed and we have to tell you that you have a rare form of leukaemia.'

'But I feel fine and surely don't I look fine. There must be some mistake.'

'Regretfully, Eammon, there is no mistake, but fortunately we seemed to have detected this early on. We need to commence treatment right away, as we don't want this to be a virulent strain.'

'A virulent strain. Christ Almighty, just what have I got?'

'Eammon, we need your approval to start treatment immediately.'

'Yes, yes you have it, but what is going to happen to me. Am I going to die?'

'One step at a time, Eammon, let us just start to contain things.'

It was now that Eammon could no longer contain himself and he burst forth all his emotion with an open bout of uncontrollable sobbing. And as the specialist tried to console him, he no longer wanted to know what the eventual outcome might be and he therefore remained silent.

Although his mind was numb and his senses shook to the core, he was still a calculating specimen and he forced himself to think clearly through the emotional turmoil. He was never a person to leave anything to chance. He planned everything with meticulous care. He looked at the sign above the door Lever & Co (solicitors/advocates). His watch revealed it was 12.30 as he spoke to the receptionist.

'Ah, Mr Dunphy. Mr Lever is waiting for you,' and he was ushered into the large spacious office.

'Eammon, tis good to see you. How are things?'

'Not so grand, Peter, that is why I am here,' he whispered faintly.

Eammon recounted his grim tale and finished by saying :-

'So now I want to make a will in the event of something nasty happening.' It took Peter Lever a good hour to draft the finer points, which in essence left all of his assets, cash, stocks and shares to his forthcoming offspring (boy or girl) that was about to be borne by one Teresa Corr his common law wife. Teresa Corr was to be appointed as trustee of the funds and to Teresa herself, he left his main residence on the condition that she and the forthcoming child reside there until the child reached the age of 16. The cash, stocks and shares were to the order of £650k and the property valued at £200k a considerable sum in all and one which was not to be sneezed at by any young mother to be.

As the days grew shorter and the nights became colder, Teresa grew stronger and her child grew with her, but Eammon was beginning to slowly ebb away. The treatment ravaged his already weakened body and he now looked a shadow of the man he once was. He knew it was time to call a meeting.

Teresa now heavily pregnant was ushered into his private dormitory. Tears trickled down her face as she gazed on the frail specimen before her. Eammon started.

'Things are not looking good and I want you to know that I love you very much. Should things not work out as we planned, you are both well catered for. Just speak to Peter Lever and he will sort everything out. The terms and conditions are pretty straightforward.' But Teresa was unable to take all this sorrow on board.

'Eammon, I will come back when you are feeling stronger,' and she quickly left the room unable to contain her emotion. It was the last time they spoke together because his weary body was unable to cope with both the illness and treatment. He expired two days later.

Dermott noticed that his requests were always answered, usually in a timely fashion. The only downside was that there was always despondency, gloom and despair attached to each major event. Unsure as to whether his master decreed that this should be so, he would just have to learn to live with this fact. After all, he was hell bent on revenge and the companions of revenge were unhappiness and sorrow. Now he heard a whisper from his subconscious. It would be very likely that Teresa and the child would now be his. His main adversary had been removed almost without warning, and the path of destruction which he followed, was enabling him to crush his enemies one by one. He mulled the thing over in his mind and mentally ticked off the names on his execution list :- Sean Farrelly, Bernard Brutton, Patrick Mahoney, Eammon Dunphy. Only Michael Flanders. remained. It was now time to cement the future with Teresa.

Chapter Twenty Two

The scene was a depressing sight; grown people in tears by the graveside, grey clouds in the sky and the priest standing in black vestments, adding to the gloom of the situation. The priest recited the last few words and then the mourners dropped earth on to the coffin, the final parting symbol of a Catholic burial. The funeral cars proceeded slowly back to Josie's house and a dozen or so people filed into the home trying to comfort Teresa and each other at the same time.

It was some time before Dermott plucked up the courage to speak with Teresa.

'What are you going to do now?' he whispered.

'It is all so confusing, I feel as though I have betrayed Eammon. I don't know what to do to put it right.'

'Do you want me to come over here?' Dermott whispered.

'I don't know what I want right now. Let's just leave it for a month or so until I can think more clearly.'

'Don't leave it too long, the baby will be here soon…….' It was at that moment that Josie interrupted.

'Teresa don't be overdoing things, you look exhausted already.'

'I am ok, mother, just need some rest,' and with that comment Teresa and Dermott had to end their brief consultation for fear of being overheard.

Two months elapsed since the passing of Eammon and Teresa and Dermott had spoken several times on the telephone, but he had not raised the subject of a future together. He would wait for Teresa to approach him.

It was January again and a cold frosty winter's morning.

His office telephone rang, it was Teresa.

'Dermott, would it be still possible for you to move over here?'

'You know it would.'

'Yes but I would want you to find your own place at least for the time being. It just would not be right, for you, me and the baby, to be together immediately.' He didn't like this last remark.

'But the baby is ours.'

'Yes but the world doesn't know that. Will you be in a position to find a job?'

'Don't worry, I am more or less a specialist consultant anyway. I can work from here as well as residing over there. Leave it all with me.........'

Once again, he felt like the Mighty Avenger. He believed his quest was to crush his enemies and lead Teresa and his child to a glorious destiny. A singular thought crossed his mind about investigating Satanic rights and ceremonies, but just for now he shelved this thought.

His pressing need was to address the mystery surrounding himself and Teresa. How was he to explain to Teresa that they were brother and sister? Once more his thoughts turned to the unborn child. Would this child inherit all his traits? Perish the thought. Thus it was that several weeks later he found himself a rented whitewashed cottage in a small village of Kildare just north of Dublin. He was once again beginning to feel proud of himself and was enjoying the control he exercised over his enemies, but Teresa's iron constitution showed some symptoms of giving way in the face of the constant stress she had been placed under. She had been to the hospital for a routine check, and more blood tests were carried out. Everything was normal but the specialist had noted her blood group as Rhesus negative and that her unborn child was Rhesus positive. He was thinking that this may cause future problems and decided to take action on this matter. He opened the cabinet containing all the medical records for Teresa and remembered that there was an addendum to her file, which referred to Eammon Dunphy. Carefully extracting the notes, his mind was trying to unravel something, but he wasn't sure what it was. He glanced slowly over the notes appertaining to Eammon. Something was troubling him. What was it? He was trying to fathom the problem but he couldn't. He would wait for the consultant to arrive later in the day, but right now he was puzzled and felt that he had missed something. All morning he was consumed with confusion then this feeling turned to guilt and then fear. Why should he be fearful? What was his problem? At first it was a slow process, but then his mind was bombarded as if he had been struck by a series of electrical convulsions. He was gripped by a paroxysm of fear, as he realised he had missed something, something vital. Checking and re-checking the file notes a second and third time, he realised that Eammon Dunphy could not be the father of Teresa's unborn child. The blood groups just did not match up. What was he to do now? He was concerned that he had mis-diagnosed some of the information. But he re-assured himself with the fact that no harm had been done to anyone. At 4pm the senior consultant confirmed his *own* findings. Now someone had to impart this information to Teresa. A week later on the morning of the meeting Teresa entered the oak-panelled office, where behind the desk sat the specialist and senior consultant. The specialist had risen from his chair and was standing between the parted blinds, gazing down into the dull neutral-tinted Dublin street. He looked and felt uncomfortable. The senior consultant welcomed her with the easy courtesy for which he was remarkable, and having closed the door and bowed her into a chair, he looked her over in the minute and yet abstract fashion which was peculiar to him. Teresa spoke first.

'Why did you wish to consult me in such a hurry Doctor? Tis only a short while since I spoke with you last.'

'Teresa, I will get to the point, there are two things. The first, which is simpler than the second, is that your child has a different blood group from your own and we will need to administer several injections to you, before your baby is born. This will prevent problems in the future should you ever become pregnant again. If we don't administer this and you do become pregnant again in the future, there would be the possibility of your second child contracting haemolytic anaemia. Quite a normal practice and nothing that you should be concerned about.'

'Well I am sure there was no need to bring me in to tell me that, I have every faith in your team. What was the second point?'

The senior consultant shifted in his seat. 'Yes, well, that is more of a personal nature so to speak.'

Teresa stirred. 'A personal nature, what exactly do you mean?'

'Teresa this is rather difficult for me, I don't quite know how to put this.' There was a pause, which seemed like an eternity.

'Your child, Teresa, cannot possibly belong to Eammon.'

'What are you saying?'

'Teresa, we have checked and re-checked yours, your child's and the blood groups taken from Eammon. Eammon could not have been the father of your child.'

As Teresa tried to speak, tears chased each other down her pale cheeks and the unhappy woman's heart was almost to breaking, as memory recalled the changeful events of her life. She sobbed some words, which were almost inaudible.

'It usually happens that a first fault, destroys the prospects of a whole life and I cannot, no I am unable to speak any further on this subject, it is too painful, you will have to forgive me..........' and she rose to leave the room.

'Teresa, if you wish to talk to us, you know where to find us, just be sure to attend for your regular check ups, and with that, the consultant leaned over to his colleague and continued debating over the comments he had just heard from his patient.

Teresa had hardly sat down when Dermott appeared at the end of the street. The worn out cobbles were now old acquaintances of his and indeed of Teresa, for they had used this wine bar often in recent times. At the end of the passage, was seen a little garden, bathed in sunshine and rich in warm and light-it was in this garden that he found Teresa sat waiting for him. It was more like a hidden garden, away from the throngs of people that paraded through the main part of the building. Teresa was seated with her head bowed when Dermott joined her. He sensed something was amiss and extending his arm she grasped his hand and motioned him to sit down. She was whispering.

'Dermott, they know at the hospital.'
'Who knows? What?'
'They know the baby is not Eammon's.' His cheeks began to colour up and now he was whispering too.
'How has this come about?'
'A routine blood check, that was all. They told me the baby could not possibly be Eammon's because of his blood group, mine and the child's.' Dermott looked thoughtfully at his lover.
'Did they ask who the father was?'
'No and I said it was a private matter or words to that effect. There are only the two of us who know.'

Dermott thought about his next statement very carefully. 'If in time we moved in together I could well, so to speak, adopt our baby. That way no one would realise, not even Josie,' but as soon as the words left his lips he cursed inwardly, because not only had the two lovers a secret to keep, but he also had one of his own. This secret he wanted to share with his true love but he kept faltering, frightened of the tragic consequences that might unfold themselves. For once he felt his wicked powers failing him.

'Let's wait until after the birth, say six months maybe, although I am unsure what Josie will say on the matter. She seems to want to keep us apart. She hasn't said as much, it is just the vibes I pick up. She seems to think we are too close already. Well we are not that close are we? I mean 2nd cousins.........'

This was Dermott's chance to break the news once and for all. He started his sentence.

'Teresa, there is something I have been meaning to tell you, but I haven't managed to get round to it. It's about the two of us.' Teresa's ears pricked up. Dermott continued.

'Teresa, I have found............ I've found exactly the same problem with Shelagh. She seems to want to keep us apart for some reason. Says we are too close. I have noticed quite a few times. At first, I thought it was because she wanted me to become a priest, but there is something more than that. Why should they both act that way towards us?'

'Well, they are sisters and they sort of think the same way, that is all I can imagine. After all, they are quite close.' And once more Dermott had lost the opportunity to reveal his findings and a force that threatened to lead him down a slippery slope and into the abyss below was slowly consuming him!

It was the latter days of February and the gales had set in with exceptional violence. All the day the wind had screamed and the rain had beaten against the hospital windows when Teresa went into a long and difficult labour. To Teresa the elements seemed to reinforce the fact that this would be a difficult time for her and eventually after a torrid struggle, with complications she gave birth to a boy Simon. The child appeared healthy enough at birth but within a week or so had to be kept on a ventilator until it gained sufficient strength of its own. The medical officials also referred to the fact that the boy may develop pes cavus of the left foot as the joints and bones developed. Dermott asked Teresa to ask for an explanation in plain English. They were duly informed that this was characterised by excessively high arches of the foot and was correctable by surgical means in severe cases. Teresa was further informed that this was no cause for concern, a fact she believed until one day she looked up the term in a medical manual. They were both dumfounded as this medical condition had another name *Claw Foot.* Now Dermott wondered what sort of being he had let loose on the earth!

Chapter Twenty Three

Dermott was becoming a very accomplished schemer, an organiser of deviltry with a controlling brain, a brain that could have made or marred the destiny of nations. Certainly, his actions had marred the lives of several who had come into contact with him and now he was hell bent on extinguishing the life of Michael Flanders, in a similar way to the fate that had befallen Patrick Mahoney. Winter was here once more. Almost one year had elapsed since the birth of his child. How quickly time moved on.

The procedures for compiling and distribution while disciplined and regimental were still open to flaw, if Dermott put his mind to it. He had perfected the timing and execution of his task to great precision. While Bradstreet was out of the room, or otherwise engaged, he once again put his plan into action. But as with all evil doers, he was becoming over confident of his own capabilities – almost arrogant. He was so sure that his master would not let him fail. But Satan's own failing had been his pride and it was possible that one of his disciples would make the same fatal mistake.

He had been asked to give a quarterly report on the progress of the 'volunteers' to the Medical Council and indeed, the members of that council had been most impressed by the satisfactory progress of the 'volunteers' except for the late Patrick Mahoney. Never before had such inroads been made with the horrific virus. Inwardly, Dermott was glowing with pride, but not the pride of success, but the pride of vanity. He had been controlling the destiny of several people and was making his mark in his unsavoury trade. Always careful in covering his tracks he was about to be *wounded* through carelessness. He thought his impregnable armour had no weakness. But it had. Now he was being asked to give regular talks on the treatment of AIDS on a national basis. He was becoming renowned as the expert in this field. It was just a matter of time before the television cameras beckoned.

The call came a week before he was to *move in* with Teresa and their child, who was now 11 months old. He had been careful not to cause undue attention to his relationship with Teresa, for fear of nagging tongues and any ensuing repercussion. A request from a major television channel to hear him deliver his *piece de resistance* had been met with careful consideration. But his calculating pride had now got the better of him. For one fleeting moment he thought about Michael Flanders but then dismissed the thought as insignificant trivia. 'Remember,' he told himself, 'I carry the number 666 which to date has proved infallible.'

The audience took their place in the midst of a profound silence. Everyone looked at Dermott with general admiration as he cast a tranquil glance around him. Dermott delivered his talk and had never been so concise and eloquent, all this in front of the gazing cameras. He looked directly into the lens, to ensure the spectators caught a full glimpse of him in his glory. With a smiling face and a heart of marble he would milk the situation until it had drained dry, explaining to the audience that together they would beat the AIDS virus. 210 miles away in the Cumbrian hills, was a spectator he could well do without. This spectator was riveted on Dermott alone and he also was placing himself in the hands of *his* avenging GOD. He uttered a long murmur of astonishment and wondered why his late friend, Patrick, had ceased to be in the land of the living, while he himself, was coping with his illness extraordinarily well. It was the first time he had discovered that Dermott Murray had been involved with the trialists!

Michael Flanders was also a thinker and retired to his study to contemplate his future. He also had a GOD and this was not a satanic god, but his own calculating mind. He retired daily to meditate and felt rejuvenated after each meditation.

He told himself that he must be blind not to have reasoned that something suspicious had happened to his friend Patrick. But how was he to test his theory out?

His recovery had been extraordinary and as far as he knew, he had been on the same medication as Patrick. All day long as he walked around, he turned the situation over in his mind, but found no explanation, which appeared to be adequate. Then he convinced himself that foul play was afoot. If he were correct, then it would only be a matter of time before he would suffer a similar fate. He made an instant decision. He would stop taking his medication for six months and give it to a stray cat that had been foraging daily for food, for the last two months. And he would start tomorrow.

Michael Flanders broke his tablet into two pieces then crushed the remains into a white powder and mixed this in with the cat food. The cat only came in the evenings and he watched as the black creature scoffed the contents of the plate without hesitation and settled down in front of the fire for a long slumber. By the time Michael Flanders rose early next morning, his adopted pet had long since departed, apparently without any nasty side effects, for the creature returned later that evening and settled back into its normal routine. Michael Flanders doubted his convictions because the creature did not appear to be suffering any ill effects whatsoever. One day, six months after the start of this routine however, the contorted features of the animal lay before him. It was an awful sight, one that brought tears to his eyes. The poor creature looked as if it had seen a ghost, so rigid was the body and so glazed were the eyes. Those eyes, which looked as if the devil himself had appeared as in an apparition. Desperate times called for desperate measures. He scooped up the stiff carcass and placed it in the cat basket, covered the body and reached for the telephone directory. He then thumbed methodically through the index until he reached the letter G. Carefully combing the entries he came upon Government Departments. Searching for several minutes he found the entry he wanted and then wrote down the telephone number of the Public Analyst.

Chapter Twenty Four

Dermott inhaled the salt breezes that blew in off the sea, as he walked back to his new home or to be more precise, *their* new home, the one that Teresa had inherited. It was a fair sized property, standing back from the road, with a curving drive, which was banked by evergreen shrubs. The blotched and weather stained door creaked as he entered, but the interior of the property was furnished like a mini-palace with marble flooring and mahogany furniture which had been requested by Eammon, before his untimely death. Expensive paintings adorned the walls and every room had been tastefully restored to its original glory. Dermott sank into the velvet armchair and began to reflect how events had taken a turn for the better, to meet his own selfish designs. The home centred interests which rise up around a man who finds himself master of his own establishment, were sufficient to absorb most of Dermott's attention. When he was not caring for Teresa and Simon he remained buried among his books and private thoughts. But beneath his calm exterior, he was fired by the fierce energy of his own nature. If he did not keep his evil plans under control he would become consumed and eventually destroyed by them. Providence had allowed him to rise from the depths of despair to newfound heights. He now had everything his heart desired. A home, and more importantly the love of Teresa, and a very good job. Why not be content? But a man like Dermott could never be content. Some hidden force drove him on and his immense faculties and powers only served for him to feast on his lust for evil. He was totally consumed! And for now, the world still was unaware that he and Teresa, were living together. The two lovers were always careful to conceal this matter from Josie, and Dermott kept a rented property not many miles away where he could return to in times of emergency. The perfect hideaway.

He recorded the months and days they had been together in a secret diary. Six months elapsed and then six months and six days. Returned to the confines of his laboratory, he deliberately watched the hands of the clock ticking round to 11.15am.

'Fancy a coffee Bradstreet?'

'Yes I'll fetch them. Your usual Dermott?'

'Yes please.'

The clock moved slowly passed the appointed hour. It was now six months, six days and six hours since he and Teresa had set up home. As a symbol of defiance he now decided to increase the strength of the death cocktail. 'Mmm, Flanders must be made of sterner stuff,' muttered Dermott and he increased the *coniine* strength by another millionth of a measure.

Dermott felt he had never been in more better mental or physical form than the June of that year. On the 6th of June, he had reason to celebrate yet another birthday and a succession of speeches and the publication of a book now enabled him to lay claim to large financial reward. But he was about to be wounded by his own genetics.

The doctor gazed across at Teresa with a look of both warmth and pity, and he began.

'Teresa, I want you to cushion yourself for what I am about to say next.' Teresa turned pale.

'Your son, Simon, has a genetic disorder.'

'A genetic disorder, how is that possible?'

'Well, for some reason, Simon has a condition called thalassaemia. This condition is normally caused by abnormal genes and is usually passed from parent to child. It is particularly common when first or second cousins wish to have children together, then there is a one in eight chance of the condition developing.' Teresa began to feel her cheeks flushing and coughed in an effort to deflect the conversation.

'Is it treatable, this condition?'

'Well, people with this condition are unable to make enough haemoglobin and the red cells are very pale. Normally, if the sufferer inherits the defect from both parents, then severe anaemia usually develops and death could occur in childhood.' Teresa gripped the chair more tightly in an effort to stay calm. The doctor continued. 'There is also another complication.........' he paused before continuing, 'your child also has a mental problem.' The pent up emotion now burst forth and Teresa began sobbing uncontrollably. It was a good ten minutes before she recovered her composure.

'What are the causes of these illnesses?'

'Teresa, they are not actually illnesses, more like genetic defects.

The normal chances of such things developing are about one in 40. If, however, two people having children are more closely related than normal, for example as I mentioned earlier, say cousins, then the chances are that much greater.' Now there was a pause as if neither of them knew what to say next. The doctor spoke first but with total innocence.

'Are you particularly close to your partner, Teresa?'

She thought carefully before answering for fear of implicating herself.

'Well, he passed away just before we were to be married. He had leukaemia.' She thought quickly of something to say next hoping it would sound sensible. 'Are leukaemia and anaemia connected?'

'No they are not and as I say, these are genetic disorders. The mental condition is a distant cousin to autism, which means Simon has a disregard of externally reality. Once again, this usually comes about if both parents are very closely related. Anyway, we will have to refer you back to your specialist as he has all your case notes.'

On hearing this, Teresa almost collapsed and had to hold on to her chair for support. My God, she thought, the specialist already knows too much. He knows Eammon is not the father and she wondered what sort of inquisition she could expect next time.

The specialist replaced Teresa's notes into the lever arch file, closed his office door and made his way into the night. A vague feeling of impending misfortune, impressed on his very being. By the time he retired, it was past midnight but he was unable to sleep for some reason. It was supposed to be summer but the wind was howling outside and the rain was beating and splashing against the windows. Suddenly, amid all the hubbub of the gale, he burst forth a shriek and he shot upright in the bed.

'My God,' he yelled. Something had been at the back of his mind for a while. Something had been troubling him and now it dawned upon him. He had been under some strain due to pressure of work but he cursed himself inwardly for being so distracted not to have noticed the glaring facts before him. In his hour of need, Eammon had asked one of his colleagues to act as a witness on the will that had been drawn up. His colleague was a meticulous person and was sure to have read the document with great care before signing as witness. The latest fragment of information, which had been, added to Teresa's file, served to re-inforce what he already knew.

Eammon had not been the biological father of Teresa's child. Of this fact, he was certain. Without doubt, these facts would have repercussions surrounding the validity of the will. He had no wish to injure Teresa in any way whatsoever, but, as a God fearing man, he had a duty to protect the innocence of the dead. The streets of Dublin were bustling with people as the specialist reached his office. Up on the third floor, his colleague Seamus O'Malley was hard at work.

'Ah, good morning Seamus, could I have a word?'

'To be sure David, what about?'

'Seamus, you remember Teresa Corr?'

'I do indeed.'

'Didn't you act as witness for her husband's will?'

'Well, they were to be married but events put an end to that.'

'Seamus, I would like you to read the file notes when you have a minute, even though you are not totally at home with the history. But before you, do let me tell you that you will be in for a shock and what is more, I think you will agree that the document you witnessed will be invalid.'

'Invalid, but how?'

'Well, please read the file notes first and then let us have a chat.'

'No problem, I will do it now.' Shaking his head in despair he read and re-read the file. He turned to David in total dismay.

'David, this is serious. I categorically remember the will stating the beneficiaries were Teresa and Eammon's offspring. These facts seriously affect matters.'

'What must we do now?'

'Well it is our duty to inform the advocate and let him sort it out.'

The advocate's face faded into an expression of intense interest and concentration as he gazed across the desk and smiled at Teresa. Her one time beautiful complexion was beginning to show signs of stress following the events of the recent weeks and she found it difficult to concentrate on what was being said. The advocate began.

'Teresa, I have some difficult news for you.' An involuntary shudder passed through her whole being. How many more times would she hear these dreadful words? 'What is happening to me?' she asked herself.

'It can't be any more difficult than the last piece of news,' she replied. The advocate spoke again, this time in a manner more akin to a barrister addressing a client in court. 'It is my sad duty to inform you, that you are not actually a true beneficiary under the terms of the late Eammon Dunphy's will.' The blood drained from her cheeks and she almost fainted.

'What on earth do you mean?'

'Teresa, it has been brought to my attention by the medical authorities, that your son Simon could not possibly have been conceived through your alliance with Eammon Dunphy.'

'And what right do the medical authorities have to reveal confidential information to anyone relating to me or my son?'

'Teresa, under common law they have every right? Seamus O'Malley was actually a witness to the will.'

'Yes but....'

The advocate intervened. 'Teresa, let me continue. The terms of the will implicitly state that your son is beneficiary of the will and that you act as trustee. That however, is assuming that Simon is the natural offspring of Eammon, which according to your specialist he is not. This also throws some doubt on the property *you* have inherited.' Teresa felt a dreadful spasm dart through her heart.

'But this is all I have left in the world, if you deprive me of that, you take away my life also.'

'Teresa, I am afraid there is nothing I can do for you on this matter.'

'What will happen now?'

'There will have to be a hearing to resolve this matter and I am obliged to put the wheels in motion today. In the meantime, your capacity to act as trustee will have to be suspended.' Teresa's normally phlegmatic disposition was collapsing under the stress.

'Just how am I and Simon and I going to survive?'

A dull, gloomy silence, like that which precedes some awful phenomenon of nature, pervaded the room and Teresa shuddered in dismay.

The bitter cup of adversity had drained Teresa to the very dregs over the previous week so badly that she had not yet brought herself to speak with Dermott about the great weight that was now crushing her. Having said that, he had not been around for a discussion, for he was back on the mainland weaving his wand of evil. Every nerve was strained, every vein was swollen and every part of her body seemed to suffer distinctly from the rest, thus, multiplying her agony a thousand fold. Dermott, stepping into the house, heard a sigh almost resembling a deep sob: he looked in the direction from where it came, and there on the velvet couch he perceived Teresa seated, with her head bowed and weeping bitterly. He looked at her face that had once radiated beauty. Her cheeks were now puffed and her eyes swollen from crying.

'Teresa, my love, what is the matter?'

'Dermott, we have got all sorts of problems.'

'Problems, what problems?'

'Dermott, I told you the specialist knew about Simon.'

'Yes but no one knows *we* made Simon.'

'No but the specialist has told the advocate and now the will is invalid.'

'The will………… told him what?'

'Dermott, a man named Seamus O'Malley who is a colleague of the specialist, was a witness to Eammon's will. They both know Eammon was not the father because of the blood groups. And now they are suggesting the real father, is closely related to me.' Had a thunderbolt struck Dermott he could not have been more stupefied! His face became ashen and he fell into a chair clutching the armrests for support. He was unsure that he had heard correctly. This was sufficient to unseat his reason. He struggled to find some words.

'What do they mean by more closely related?' Teresa now burst into uncontrollable sobbing.

'Dermott, our baby has some form of genetical defect that is normally common, if the parents are closely related. Dermott, I knew we should have never got involved.' Dermott was wounded and his armour was weakening by the seconds.

'I still don't know what they mean by closely related.'

'They said the genetical defects, are more normally found in children whose parents are first or second cousins or closer.'

'Defects, you said defects. Simon has more than one defect?'

'Dermott, he has a condition called thalassaemia, and if he has inherited this from both of us, there is a fair chance he will die in childhood and worse than that, he has another condition, I can't remember the name of it right now, which means he is not in touch with reality. He is totally self absorbed.' On hearing these words, Dermott collapsed into a fit of uncontrollable sobbing and at the same time felt the muscles round his heart tighten. The whole event sent him into a spasmodic panic attack. His mind was racing from his evil deeds, to his avenging God and then back to Teresa and then to Simon, and he truly felt he was destined to walk the earth as an evil, no good son of the devil. He knew he was responsible for the dreadful condition of his son Simon and was convinced his issue would also be a devil's disciple. Never had there been more urgency to tell Teresa about the secret he had discovered, but right now that would only make matters worse, because the tears chased down her wan cheeks and her heart was embittered, as she cried herself to sleep still wondering why these misfortunes had befallen her.

Chapter Twenty Five

Peter Lever the advocate, Teresa, the specialist and Seamus O'Malley took their places in the most profound silence; the commissioner dealing with the case entered the room. The information that had been supplied by the specialist and his colleague and verified by the hospital had been translated onto formal printed legal documents. The commissioner explained to the specialist and Seamus O'Malley, that before singing them they ought to be completely satisfied that the details in the forms were true in every respect. As contestants, theirs was the responsibility that everything was completely and accurately stated. They carefully went through each part of the oath and account, which tallied exactly with the information supplied. Satisfied everything was in order, they signed the oath in the space provided at the end. The oath contained a clause identifying the original will and declaring it null and void due to the fact that Eammon Dunphy could not have been the biological father of Simon Corr. The commissioner then finished by stating that the Public Trustee was to be appointed as executor and all assets and the property were to pass under this jurisdiction, to be eventually divided amongst the family members of the late Eammon Dunphy.

Teresa let out a piercing cry, ending in a sob and fell into a fit of hysterics.

'My beautiful home, where am I going to live, how can I support my demented child? What have I done to deserve this torment?' And she had to be supported by the medical pair as they left the commissioner's office.

It was a hot summer evening and the thermometer was still in the late 70s and the conversation, which had roamed in a desultory fashion from health and fitness came round at last, to the question of atavism and hereditary aptitudes. Teresa tackled the subject first. 'Dermott, Simon must have inherited the faulty genes from either one of us or indeed both of us. The hospital, are asking me to disclose your identity in order that they can more easily carry out tests, which in the long term may help Simon. Without both sets of records, they are floundering and he is now beginning to need constant care. The condition is worsening. Dermott, we have got to help him.' Her lover was about to answer when the sound of voices were heard at the front door, someone pressed the doorbell until the whole house resounded with the sound of clanging. Dermott opened the door and there stood two tall men, both dressed in jacket tie and blue shirts. The taller of the two spoke first.

'Mr Dermott Murray?' he said thrusting an identity card into Dermott's face.

'Yes,' replied Dermott.

'Inspector Gregson of the mainland police, and sergeant White from the Garda, could we have a word?' Dermott was so overwhelmed by this enormous and unexpected calamity, that he could scarcely stammer a few words as he looked at the two policemen in front of him.

'Why, yes what is this about?'

'Are you alone sir?'

'Well, actually no.'

'It will probably be better if we go down to the station then.'

'Down to the station, why is that?'

'It is a rather delicate matter, it won't take us long to get there. Could you come with us sir?'

'Well, I will just have to inform Teresa, hang on a second.'

But Teresa had heard the conversation and was now in the hallway and she beckoned Dermott to go with the officers with a look of incredulity on her face. The younger of the two detectives gazed upon Teresa, with a look of curiosity.

'It's Patricia, isn't it?'

'No my name is Teresa.'

'Oh I am so sorry, yes, Teresa……….. I am Peter White. Didn't we go to the same school, Our Lady of Sorrows?' Teresa coloured up and her embarrassment could not be hidden.

'Yes, I did go to Our Lady of Sorrows but only for two terms. I am sorry, I didn't recognise you.'

'No worry, it was such a long time ago.' Then Dermott spoke rather hurriedly.

'See you later, my love, you had better wait up for me,' and with that he walked towards the awaiting car with his escorts. The inside of the police room was hot and sticky. The inspector himself was a man of 45 years of age, tall, strong and bony, a perfect specimen of the natives of these latitudes. He had the dark, sparkling and deep-set eye, curved nose and teeth as white as those of a carnivorous animal. His naturally murky complexion had assumed a deep shade of brown and when the light fell upon his face, he looked every bit like an executioner waiting to extract the last drop of blood from his next victim.

'Dermott, thank you for your patience, we are sorry to have to drag you away from your home but certain allegations have been made and we need to talk to you about them.'

'Allegations against whom, me?'

'Dermott, you have been involved in trials with AIDS victims have you not?'

A greenish paleness spread over Dermott's cheeks and a throbbing pain in his left temple, felt as though someone was inserting a sharp instrument into the side of his head.

'Yes, I have and the trials are going very successfully.' The detective moved his chair uncomfortably closer to Dermott as if to strangle him emotionally.

'One of the volunteers died, did he not?'

'Well, yes, but he was not in the best of health, none of them are, as you can imagine and there are no guarantees of success.'

'Yes, we understand that, do you actually know what the cause of death was, Dermott?'

'Well, I am not a coroner, I merely sent his medical records to the coroner. I think it was asphyxia due to drowning. He was lost at sea.'

'Do you know anything about poisons?' There was an imposing silence.

'Yes, I come into contact with them in the course of my duty.' There was another ill-foreboding silence.

'Look, just what is this all about?'

'Dermott, do you know someone named Michael Flanders?'

A look of despair appeared in Dermott's eyes and he struggled to get his word out, like one who has been driven to the extreme limits of his reason.

'Yes, he is also one of the trialists.' There was a pregnant pause and the detective delivered the words slowly, with calculating venom.

'Dermott, you are accused by Michael Flanders of trying to deliberately poison him with the prescription you administered to him.' On hearing these imputations, Dermott felt himself on the brink of an enormous chasm that was about to swallow him up. He tried to regain composure.

'This is absolute nonsense, what proof is there?'

'Dermott, the state is to bring the charges against you of deliberately trying to poison Michael Flanders. And there may be further charges relating to the death of Patrick Mahoney in due course. Do you have anything to say before I formally charge you?'

'Where is the proof and what is the so called motive?'

'The public analyst has been involved and we are informed that there is sufficient information for us to press charges. Do you understand the seriousness of the charges?' Dermott was almost defeated.

'The public analyst? What on earth for and what motive could I possibly have for this act?'

'All in due course Dermott, do you have representation here in Ireland?'

'I do and I wish to call my advocate now.' Three hours later Dermott had been charged and was remanded in custody until someone could be found to put up the necessary bail. Once more, he found himself plunged into the depths of despair but perhaps this time his master had deserted him. There was no one available to bail him out but he found himself free by special court order, on the condition that his passport was surrendered, to prevent him leaving the Irish Shores.

As the months passed, Dermott felt a species of stupor creeping over him and now only two weeks away from his trial, he felt defeated powerless and crushed by the heavy burden he had toiled with.

Teresa looked up and fixed her eyes on Dermott.

'Look at me,' she continued with a feeling of profound melancholy. I am bowed down with fatigue, my eyes no longer sparkle, all this grief has created an abyss between the happy days and the present. I have a child leaning closely towards death's door. The man I love is now accused of some heinous crime and I am penniless. What have I done to deserve all this? Dermott, you knew Michael Flanders was a trialist. Why then did you not distance yourself from this past connection? Life would have been so much simpler.' Dermott compressed his lips as if seeking to conquer his rage, but as an accomplished liar, he rarely knew the difference between what was the truth and what was fabrication. He was practised at the art of deception and even Teresa was unable to penetrate his veil of deceit.

'This charge is a complete fabrication. All I have done is to treat him with the new vaccine. He is just hell bent on revenge and thinks this will deflect from the possibility of a perjury case. Lord knows he has been hiding behind this illness long enough. If he had been in good health, charges would have been brought by now. They soon concocted enough evidence to bring me to court. No one really expected him to be still around. But he will reap the rewards he deserves.'

'And just what rewards are those, Dermott?'

'He deserves his lot after what he and his cohorts did to me.'

'It sounds as if you are still hell bent on revenge. If you carry on in this manner, I will start believing the police are right.'

'Teresa, I have done nothing to Michael Flanders, why don't you believe me?'

'I do, but you are an angry young man and you have always wanted revenge. Why not let the courts settle his account in due course? You are getting yourself in deep water and what are we going to do with Simon? Just look at him..........' and Teresa turned to look at the pale, sickly looking introverted shaking specimen lying on the couch in Dermott's cottage and once more, she burst into tears. The pressure was mounting on Dermott and he was finding it hard to contain. He fully realised the problem and consequences that had arisen from his failure to tell Teresa of his secret. He tried to move the subject away from Simon back onto Teresa's family.

Tentatively he asked. 'What does Josie have to say about Simon's illness?'

'What does she say? She says that I have been the unluckiest person in the world. First Simon loses his father and then he is born with these defects.' Dermott interjected.

'But he hasn't lost his father.'

'Well, you and I know that but Josie doesn't. And she still doesn't know about the will. I haven't had the courage to tell her and the hospital want you to come forward. They need a blood sample and some knowledge of your medical records. They say it will help with Simon's treatment and up to now I have told them nothing but I can't keep making excuses. They need to know. We must go to the hospital and let them carry out whatever tests they need to. We owe it to Simon.' Dermott was defeated. He had to comply with Teresa's request. But as usual he tried to deflect the blame away from himself and bring another person into the drama.

'Won't they need to test Josie and your father, too? The more information they have, the easier it must be to diagnose the problem.'

'Dermott, it is the parent's they need to examine, you and I, not the grandparents and I have told you before, I don't know where my father is. Josie says we are better off without him, he is a bad lot.'

'Perhaps the genetic defect is on his side then.'

'Dermott, I am the mother and you are the father, let's have the test done and leave it at that. Will you please attend the hospital so that we can help Simon?'

'But I don't really see what can be achieved, all they might find is that we are cousins and *we* already know that.'

'If it means we can help Simon then it is worth it. What have we got to hide, I don't understand your reluctance.'

'Okay, I will go straight after the trial.'

'No, Dermott, you will go before the trial. Have you considered that you might not get off.'

'That is nonsense, there is no evidence against me. I am sure to get off. I know what I have done and what I haven't. Flanders just wants to seek his revenge because he is dying and I am free. He is angry because misfortune has overtaken him in the form of this dreadful disease and the possibility of an eventual trial.' But in Dermott's case, if he didn't face the hospital specialist, he would have to face the court in the very near future.

Chapter Twenty Six

Dermott's puckered eyelids began to quiver as he listened to the recital of his counsel and his vacant blue eyes looked up with a stare that indicated he was not taking it all in. Some of the facts were going above his head. He could not believe that the charges were levied at *him*.

'Now, Dermott, let us go through this once more. You are accused by Michael Flanders of administering a substance, contained in the prescription of the said Michael Flanders, with the sole intention of endeavouring to cause injury or death by poisoning. Do you understand the charge?'

'Yes, but there is no evidence, no motive and all the prescriptions were administered under strict supervision of the Medical Council.'

'Let me go through this again. Flanders says your motive was to obtain retribution for his damming evidence against you in your earlier trial. The prosecution must have sufficient evidence to have brought the case to trial.'

'How can someone who is on charge for perjury bring another case into the arena?'

'Dermott, you must face up to the facts. The law has allowed this to happen and it will go ahead and we must prepare diligently. The jury may well consider you had a motive. The prosecuting counsel will have to find evidence of poisoning and you say the drugs were issued under strict control. It is not a very strong case from my experience and of course you are pleading not guilty,' and with that, Dermott nodded his agreement and tried to concentrate on what he was supposed to say.

The trial of Dermott Murray, in November 1992 for the attempted poisoning of Michael Flanders was to create an exceptional amount of public attention. The press, were in particularly nasty form, behaving like vultures picking at every morsel they could find, to enhance their *own exclusive.* Dermott convinced himself he was in fine fettle, vehemently denying the charge *as a waste of the authorities' time* until six days before the trial was to begin, the press got a hold of a real exclusive. A paroxysm of fear shook his body rigid when he read the banner headline 'BODY OF AIDS TRIALIST TO BE EXHUMED'.

Dermott's counsel spoke with a grave voice. 'Dermott, I regret to inform you that the authorities have now got permission to exhume Patrick Mahoney's body and it is very likely you will face a second charge of some sort should they find anything untoward. As for who released this information to the press, I do not know, it certainly wasn't me.'

From very early in the morning, a crowd gathered at Liverpool Crown court, some to witness the trial, others to comment on it. It was a sad spectacle indeed that there was standing room only to witness the gloomy proceedings. Patrick Cusack in his opening speech, on behalf of Michael Flanders, outlined the history of the case. He pointed out that it had to be shown first, that poison had been deliberately introduced into Michael Flanders' prescription, for the sole purpose of causing injury or death. Secondly, it had to be shown without doubt that Dermott Murray was the person who had administered the poison. He contended that the accused had used his special knowledge of poisons, to interfere with the prescription in a manner likely to cause injury or death to Michael Flanders.

Dermott's counsel felt that with regard to the two charges the odds were 85% - 15% firmly in his favour. The evidence for the prosecution was given first.

Michael Flanders took to the stand and once the preliminary formalities were out of the way, Peter Cusack began.

'Mr Flanders, would you please tell the members of the jury how you first came to know the accused?'

He started tentatively. 'I first met Dermott Murray at the seminary, Loyola Hall in 1985, when we were studying for the priesthood.'

'And tell me, did you get on well with Mr Murray?'

'Yes, at first I did.'

'How well? Would you say you were close or just good friends?'

'I would say at the time we were good friends.'

'And did this friendship flourish over the course of time?'

'For a period yes, until about 1987 when there was a hiccup.'

'A hiccup you say. So do we take it you fell out?'

'Yes, that is correct.'

'You fell out and why did you fall out?'

Michael Flanders stammered and seemed unable to find any

words.

'Well, it was a delicate matter.'

'A delicate matter, what exactly do you mean by that?'

'Well he was accused of indecent assault against one of our brothers and he was convinced this was down to me.'

'And was it down to you?'

'No, brother Sean brought the charges, I merely gave my opinion of what actually took place.'

'I see and what was the outcome of the charge?'

'He was eventually convicted of the charge.'

'I see, so do we concur that from this moment on, Dermott Murray had every reason to dislike you?'

'Yes, that is correct.'

'And in your opinion, was that dislike tantamount to hatred?'

The defence counsel interjected.

'Objection, your honour, the prosecution is leading the witness down that line of thought.'

'Objection overruled. Continue with your witness.'

Flanders paused. 'Yes in my opinion he has hated me ever since then, because he feels I was partly to blame for his conviction.'

'Hated you enough to poison you?'

'Objection, your honour.'

'Objection overruled, continue.'

'Yes, I am convinced he wanted to poison me in retribution.'

'So he tampered with your prescription. Would you please explain what you are being treated for?'

Flanders gripped the dock more tightly.

'I have the AIDS virus and I am being treated for that.'

'And would you please tell the members of the jury how the accused came to be the person to administer your prescription.'

'The accused is a leading authority on the treatment of AIDS and I am one of several people involved with trials of a new drug.'

'I see and has this new drug been of benefit to you?'

'Well, yes, I think so, but quite a while back, I became suspicious that my medication was being tampered with.'

'Mr Flanders, would you please tell us, what aroused your suspicion?'

'To begin with, I didn't realise that Dermott Murray was involved with this research. But then one day, I saw him deliver a talk on television, about his work and success with the virus. It was then that I became suspicious.'

'Why, because he gave a talk on the subject?'

'No, it was because a former colleague from the seminary, was also receiving treatment for the same virus and he died.' Stifled whispers could be heard from the public gallery.

'He died, you say?'

'Yes.'

'Of what did he die?'

'Objection, your honour, the witness is not a coroner.'

'Objection sustained.'

'Your honour, may my witness answer in lay man's terms?'

'Yes he may answer the question, but he must not elaborate.'

'You may answer, Mr Flanders.'

'I was told he died from the virus.'

'So this ex colleague, was he also a friend of yours?'

'Yes, a very close friend.'

'Would Dermott Murray also have reason to dislike your friend? I don't think we know his name.'

'His name was Patrick Mahoney and Dermott Murray had a good reason to hate him also.'

'Why is that?'

'Because he also gave evidence against the accused in his previous trial.' The judge spoke up.

'Mr Cusack, I shouldn't have to remind you, that reference to the late Patrick Mahoney is not related to this case.'

'I am sorry, your honour, I had no intent to mislead the jury.'

'Then continue.'

A hubbub of noise pervaded throughout the courtroom until the guilty parties were told to refrain from conversation.

'Thank you, Mr Flanders, I have no further questions on this matter. However, I wish to turn your attention to your prescription. How long have you been taking this medication?'

'I commenced taking the new drug in September 1989.'

'And you say that your health has been stable?'

'Yes, reasonably so.'

'Are you still taking this medication?'

'I stopped taking it for six months.'

'Why is that?'

'I told you, I felt sure it was poisoned.'

'Do you have any reason to support this allegation?'

'Yes, I do.'

Once more there were hushed whispers in the courtroom.

'Quiet in court.'

'Please, tell us what that is.'

'When I stopped taking the medication I gave it to my cat instead.'

'You gave it to your *cat*?'

'Yes, I wanted to see if it would affect the cat. If there were any affects, then I would have some evidence to hand.'

The courtroom became noisy once more.

'Silence in court, I will not have my court distracted!'

'Tell me, did anything happen to your *cat?*'

'Nothing at first, but after six months it passed away.'

'What was the cause of death?'

'It was poisoning.'

'How do you know it was not from natural causes?'

'Because I took the corpse to the public analyst and he confirmed it was a very strange case. He said the animal was strangely rigid and looked as if it had seen a ghost or even the devil itself.'

'Mr Flanders, I have no wish to offend you, but all creatures would be stiff after rigor mortis had set in.'

'I am only telling you what the analyst said.'

'Yes, thank you.'

Cusack then stroked his chin as if he were to say something of great importance but his next statement was almost an anti climax.

'One final question, Mr Flanders, do you intend taking the medication again?'

'Yes, I actually started taking it four days ago.'

'I assume you no longer feel that it is tainted with poison then?'

'Yes, that is correct,' and both Cusack and Flanders returned to their seats. The judge spoke next in dulcet tones.

'There will be a one-hour recess. Proceedings commence again at 2pm.' Dermott was shell shocked and totally stunned by the clarity and decisiveness of the evidence Flanders had given. He was having to fight hard to get back on his feet and it would be a long time before he himself would be called to the witness stand, because next it was the turn of the Public Analyst to be examined by Cusack.

Bang on the stroke of two o'clock the session re-convened and Cusack commenced his examination of the Public Analyst.

Chapter Twenty Seven

'Dr Taylor, would you please tell the jury what your occupation is and also your qualifications?'

'I am the Chief Public Analyst for the North of England and I am a Fellow of the College of Surgeons and a Fellow of the Society of Apothecaries. I also hold an Honours Degree issued by the Institute of Toxicology.'

'And how long have you held your current post?'

'For six years now.'

'I see, so we can assume from that, you are reasonably experienced in your chosen profession?'

'Before that, I was Senior Lecturer in medicine at Christ's College Oxford.'

'Would you tell us how you came to be involved with this case and the part you have played in it?'

'One day in July, my team received a telephone call from the police informing us they were investigating a possible serious crime and that a written authority would follow, asking us to perform an autopsy, on the corpse of a cat. Apparently, Mr Flanders had called our offices enquiring of the legal procedures concerning an autopsy and had then contacted the police, whereupon from then on, they were dealing with the matter.'

'So, you were instructed to carry out an autopsy on a cat, for what purpose?'

'We were instructed to look for signs of irritant poisoning that may have caused the death of the cat.'

'Did you not think that this was a strange request at the time?'

'Maybe so, but our job is to analyse not to question the reason why.'

'Would you tell us what happened from there, Dr Taylor?'

'One of my team carried out an autopsy and as is standard practice in serious cases, I was asked to check on the findings.'

'Please continue.'

'A member of my team examined the main organs, with myself, as witness in conjunction. There was a large patch of effused blood at the cardiac end of the stomach, the rest of the mucous membrane was pale except near the pylorus. There was no ulceration. There was some inflammation at the commencement of the duodenum,' Cusack interrupted.

'I am sorry, your honour, but it could be that some members of the jury may not understand some of the medical terms used by my witness, indeed I am at a loss myself on some occasions.'

'Yes, I agree. Dr Taylor, would you be so kind as to try to use more simple terms for all our benefit, wherever you can. If that is not possible, we will just have to try to follow your narrative or ask if we are unsure. Thank you.'

'The pylorus, your honour, is the opening from the stomach to the duodenum, which itself is the first section of the small intestine.'

'Thank you Dr Taylor.'

'In the lower foot of the small intestine, the mucous membrane was very much thickened. The beginning of the large intestine was nearly destroyed by inflammation and ulceration: these appearances decreased along the colon and rectum. The only natural disease, associated with such appearances, would be dysentery but it is also possible, that irritant poisoning could cause such appearances. Included in this term, might be arsenic, antimony and corrosive sublimate. In summary, therefore, there was intense ulceration of the bowels, the only natural cause which could be acute dysentery, unless poisoning was present.'

'What was your professional opinion at this stage Dr Taylor?'

'It was too early to say, we had to look for further signs for irritant poisoning. If arsenic were present, we would expect to find a certain amount in the body.'

'And did you?'

'We examined the spleen, liver, gullet, kidneys and large and small intestines and we found no traces of arsenic whatsoever. We did, however, find a substance similar to hemlock, in the blood from the heart. There was also a minute trace in the kidneys, but due to the length of time that had elapsed since death and our autopsy, it was impossible to say for certainty what this was. It certainly resembled hemlock.'

'Would you care to furnish us with a better understanding of what hemlock is Dr Taylor?'

'Certainly, it is an oily liquid similar to nicotine but it is very poisonous, the smallest dose would be certain to cause death in a short period of time.'

'What sort of dose would be likely to cause death?'

'Well, if it were administered over a period of time, say a millionth of a measure, over an eight month period, then it would build up in the blood stream and eventually cause death. If, on the other hand, 5mg were administered in a 25mg capsule, then death would occur within about three hours.'

'Dr Taylor, where would one come into contact with this very dangerous *hemlock*?'

'Well, you certainly would not find it anywhere other than in a laboratory, where other dangerous poisons are kept.'

'So, a man or woman, or indeed an animal, would be most unlikely to accidentally stumble on this, let alone consume it.'

'Most unlikely.'

'What would you say the odds were, of accidentally consuming as poison such as this?'

'Well, I am not a mathematician but I would guess the odds are about 20 million to one.'

'Thank you.'

'Now, let us turn to the matter of the actual cause of death. Were you able to say with certainty the actual cause of death?'

'We decided that the lungs had failed and the heart was paralysed and the cause of death was asphyxia.'

'In other words, insufficient oxygen to put it in layman's terms.'

'Yes, that is correct.'

'Would you say that this hemlock in the blood stream was a contributory factor to the cause of death?'

'Most certainly so.'

'Now, we know that Mr Flanders had been feeding the cat with his medication. Therefore, let me ask you, if Mr Flander's medication had been tampered with, would it have been possible to somehow induce the hemlock into the medication, without detection and if that were the case, would the build up in the bloodstream of the animal, have been sufficient to cause death?'

'I cannot answer the first part of the question, as I do not know how the capsules are produced. But most certainly, in my opinion, if the hemlock built up over the course of time, it would be most likely be the major cause of death.'

'No further questions, your honour, but I wish to call the accused to the stand'.

'Mr Murray, I think it only fair to the members of the jury to get straight to the point. We have heard from Mr Flanders that you had very good reason not to like him. Indeed you had every reason to despise him. Would that not be a fair assessment of the facts?'

Dermott's calculating disposition had warned him not to lose his cool and be prepared for a nasty examination from Cusack. He remained calm and looked Cusack directly in the eye, which began to unnerve the interrogator, somewhat.

'I had reason to dislike him, yes. But not to despise him.' The courtroom went silent upon hearing Dermott's reply. 'So with my beliefs, I put my trust in my God and I asked for him to sort matters out, and eventually I was vindicated. Therefore, I had no reason to wish Michael Flanders any harm whatsoever. In fact, I feel very sorry for him, as he has been suffering from this dreadful virus for a while now, but we are very hopeful that we will find a cure, in the near future. I am actually hoping for his complete recovery.'

Cusack was completely taken aback with Dermott's apparent sincere and pitiful reply. Not expecting this, but expecting a war of words, he ceased to speak for a second until the judge interrupted.

'Do you wish to continue, Mr Cusack?'

'Yes, your honour. Mr Murray, what exactly do you mean, when you say you were vindicated?'

'I mean that Sean Farrelly confessed that he had been telling lies and that I was innocent.'

'But what you really mean is, you were vindicated when he passed away and when Mr Flanders here became ill. Is that not nearer to the truth?' The judge looked exasperated.

'Mr Cusack, the accused has already answered your questions regarding Mr Flanders. *Your* reference to Sean Farrelly has nothing to do with *this* case. Kindly remember that.'

'Apologies, your honour, my intention was to root out the truth not mislead.'

'We are all trying to root out the truth, that is why we are here, and you should know the correct code of conduct by now.'

'No further questions, your honour.'

Chapter Twenty Eight

Public attention was becoming intense and now the jury and those in the public gallery were waiting in eager anticipation for the defence to bring forward their witnesses. Bernard Mowbray represented Dermott, and it was usual to call the accused to the stand first, but Mowbray caused some surprise by asking if he could cross-examine Dr Taylor, the analyst, first. The judge acceded to his request.

'Dr Taylor, your work involves you in dealing with many types of poisons does it not?'

'That is correct.'

'Would you say you are an expert in this field?'

'I have to have an extensive knowledge of the subject to be able to carry out my job.'

'Have you come across any other cases similar to this one in the course of your career?'

'I spent several years working in Southern India where cases of dysentery were common. I have performed autopsies on several humans with similar diseases, but I have never carried an autopsy on an animal before.'

'Was there foul play suspected in any of the cases you dealt with?'

'In just the one case. This was a case of serious poisoning where arsenic or antimony had been administered over a long period of time.'

'In other words slow, poisoning.'

'That is correct.'

'And were your findings similar or identical to your finding in this case?'

'With arsenic and antimony it is normal to find traces in the major organs, such as the heart, liver, kidneys and also the intestines.'

'Would you expect to find traces in the tissues as well?'

'Almost certainly.'

'I see. Can we just summarise? In cases of slow poisoning then, one could expect to find elements in the heart, liver, kidneys, intestines and also the tissues of the body?'

'In most cases, but it would not be evenly distributed. But it is pretty certain that it would be in the liver and normally the tissues.'

'Yet, correct me if I am mistaken, in this particular case you found traces of a substance in only the heart and kidneys?' Once more whispers could be heard all round the courtroom and it was a good minute before the room was free from distraction.

'Yes, that is correct.'

'Can you explain then Dr Taylor, why you did not find any poison in the tissues, liver or intestines? Although the cat had some form of disease, could it not be, that it still died of natural causes?'

'As I explained, the irritant would not necessarily be evenly distributed but I cannot explain why there was no substance in the tissues, liver or intestines. But I know of no natural disease, to which I could attribute the symptoms. I believe death was caused by, irritant poisoning.'

'But you don't know how the poison was administered to the prescription, if indeed it was at all.'

'That is correct.'

'Dr Taylor, let me ask you, there is no way your autopsy could be flawed, is there not?'

Taylor was becoming angry, he took this statement as an attack on his professional pride.

'The nature of our profession is a very serious one indeed and we cannot afford to make any errors in the course of our work, particularly when a person's liberty is at stake.'

'Yes, of course. Dr Taylor would you say the standards of departments such as yours, are of the highest order throughout the UK?'

'Well, I can't speak for other departments but I can assure you that the standards of my department are second to none. Having said that, I would be pretty certain that all similar departments would maintain standards to the highest order.' Taylor's brow darkened more and more, and his white lips and clenched teeth were filled with apprehension. He could not fathom where Mowbray was leading him, but was sure he was not going to like the outcome.

'Dr Taylor, does your department use the latest technology?'

'Yes, we pride ourselves on this matter.'

'And within that sphere, you would include the instruments you use in the course of your work?'

'Quite definitely.'

'Are you aware of company by the name of PMT?' Taylor's face became ashen and he cleared his throat.

'Yes, it stands for Pioneering Medical Technology. The company is a pioneer in developing high tech hypodermic syringes. Their syringes help prevent medical professionals from contracting the AIDS virus.'

'Would you be so kind as to explain how this works?'

'In the old days, when a hypodermic needle was thrust into an organ or tissue for the purpose of extracting a liquid or substance, there was always a risk that the person using the needle, would prick himself either before or after the incision. You can imagine that this practice could be very dangerous if the liquid was contaminated with the AIDS virus because you may then infect your own blood stream, with the very virus that you are trying to treat. With this piece of equipment, the actual needle contacts into the barrel of the syringe after the incision, and therefore, as the needle is no longer protruding, all risk from a contaminated piece of equipment is eliminated.'

'Thank you for explaining it so eloquently. So, Dr Taylor, the same principle could be applied to any substance you were extracting, say hemlock for example?'

'That is correct.'

'Would you say that this company PMT was a reputable company?'

'They are an American company with years of experience in the medical market.'

'Did your department use their methods and equipment?' Taylor was beginning to sweat and shifted his feet as if to prepare for some heavy blow.

'Most of the medical departments, hospitals and universities, throughout the UK, used their research tools. It has been common practice for the last six to seven years.'

'Dr Taylor I would like to read to you and members of the jury, a copy of a memorandum from the government health minister, to all medical departments, hospitals and re-search departments in the United Kingdom and including the Republic of Ireland. It reads :-

Pioneering Medical Technology
To: Chief Executive, British Medical Council
Dated 4th January 1992

Government Health ministers have today issued the following statement. Imports of hypodermic equipment manufactured by Pioneering Medical Technology, have today ceased until such time Her Majesty's government is satisfied that a major flaw in the usage of the hypodermic syringe has been eradicated.

This instruction relates specifically to the usage of the hypodermic syringe, specially manufactured to prevent the spread of the AIDS virus. The new syringe used for injecting and extracting fluids from organs of the body has developed a major serious flaw. The needle itself is constructed from malleable plastic and nylon, which whilst very versatile has shown serious deficiencies in usage. Because of the *nature* of the components of the *needle* itself, it has been proved that on certain occasions, contact with bodily fluids can cause a malfunction, which results in a discharge of a dangerous substance into the bloodstream or organs. The release of this substance is now known to be of a serious poisonous nature. Until this malfunction has been remedied, all medical departments, hospitals and research departments (including laboratories) must refrain from the use of any equipment manufactured by Pioneering Medical Technology. The use of such technology carries a serious government health warning. Failure to adhere to this instruction will be construed as a matter of serious misconduct. It is expected that clearance will be given in due course.

All eyes turned towards the doctor in the witness box, who unable to bear the universal gaze, now riveted on him alone, gripped the stand for support.

'Dr Taylor, can you tell us if and when, your department started using the hypodermic syringe referred to in this memorandum?' Taylor was unsure what reply to offer for he did not know what evidence Mowbray had uncovered. He was under great duress to speak the truth.

A dull, gloomy silence, like that which precedes some awful phenomenon of nature, pervaded the assembly, who shuddered in dismay. Taylor was beginning to think he was no longer in possession of his senses.

He dropped his head, his teeth chattered like those of a man under an attack of fever and he was deadly pale.

'We commenced using the syringe in July last year as it was seen as a major breakthrough in this area of work and I think we stopped the use in August this year.'

'Dr Taylor, you stopped the use in August this year. That is a full eight months, after the warning was issued. I would suggest that this was an error of serious misgivings.'

'The government statement is not actually binding. It is only a recommendation, we are left to make our own decisions.'

'You are left to make your own decisions. Dr Taylor, would you not think that when you are dealing with a serious charge, which could affect the future and freedom of another human being, that you might have taken more care and paid heed to this warning?'

'We were asked to examine the dead corpse for irritant poisoning. The full facts of the case were never disclosed to us. We were totally unaware of Michael Flanders or Dermott Murray.'

'Nevertheless, I am suggesting to you that this, in most people eyes, is a serious breach of misconduct. Let me further remind you Dr Taylor, that I have evidence here, that your department carried out the autopsy as instructed on 31st July this year and that you ceased using the Pioneer Medical Technology syringes on 15th August. 15 days after you carried out the examination. Let me ask you. Do you not think that there could be some doubt as to the validity of you examination? Would it not be feasible that in view of the problems with the syringes, that this poisonous substance, in this case the hemlock, was caused by the needle coming into contact with the body fluids?' Taylor now spoke with a hoarse choking voice as he struggled to regain composure.

'I admit it is possible but it is very unlikely indeed because hemlock is a very rare poison.'

The whole assembly was dumb with astonishment at the revelation of the facts so concisely delivered by Mowbray.

'No further questions, your honour.'

Chapter Twenty Nine

Mowbray was a clever man and always researched and planned his defence with great meticulousness. He next called Dr Wright to the stand.

'Dr Wright, would you please tell us about your background and where you work?'

'I am a doctor of medicine and professor of physiology at the Cambridge School of Medicine. I specialise in the study of poisonous substances and have done so for the last ten years.'

'Dr Wright, you have acquainted yourself with the facts of this case, have you not?'

'Yes, I have.'

'And what is your opinion of the findings of the autopsy?'

'My opinion is that the evidence is not reconcilable with slow irritant poisoning. There was an absence of several points I should have expected to find. The results of the examination were against a case of poisoning of this description, as the inflammation was most developed in that part of the intestines, which in irritant poisoning, generally received the least injury. I would have expected the *coniine* or hemlock as it is commonly known as, to be found in the tissues of the body especially the liver and spleen. The same would apply to other irritant poisons such as arsenic or antimony. The evidence more resembled acute dysentery, than slow irritant poisoning. The condition of the intestines was not consistent with slow irritant poisoning. If no hemlock were found in the tissues, I would doubt that poison was the cause of death.'

'Thank you Dr Wright. A couple more questions. Have you and your colleagues ever used equipment produced by Pioneering Medical Technology?'

'Yes, we have.'

'Would that include the suspect syringes referred to by Dr Taylor.'

'Yes, we used them for a short period of time, from October last year until January this year when the warning was issued.'

'During the time you were using them, did you at any time, regard them as dangerous?'

'On one occasion, during an autopsy, we found traces of a substance similar to the substance referred to in this case. Obviously as this was an autopsy, the person had already passed away and therefore, there was no further danger to life. If we were injecting or extracting fluid to a living person the results could have been catastrophic.'

'No further questions Dr Wright.'

'The sitting is adjourned. All parties report to the court 9am tomorrow morning.'

Although Dermott secretly acknowledged his guilt, he felt protected by his grief. Through his Satanic urgencies he saw the workings of a divine hand. His only worry was not for himself but for his beloved sister and lover, Teresa. He felt that because he carried the infection of crime, Teresa might somehow become infected, as one would with the typhus fever, the cholera or even the plague. He mentally prepared himself for his next examination. Mowbray began by asking Dermott about his time at the seminary with Michael Flanders.

'Now, we have heard from Mr Flanders, that during your time at the training college, you became friends. Is that statement correct?'

'Yes, we were friends for a while.'

'Were you just acquaintances or more than that?'

'We were more than acquaintances. The close proximity of all the novices tends to bring you into contact on a daily basis and obviously a feeling of warmth is encouraged towards ones fellow man. This generally means that you make friends with most of your peers.'

'Now, we understand that there was a falling out between yourself and Mr Flanders. Was this as school pals sometimes do or was it of a more serious nature?'

'It was serious, very serious. I joined the college to study for the priesthood, not to mingle with a collection of gays.' Once more the court erupted.

'Silence, I will not have interruptions in this court.'

'Are you intimating that all the people at the college are gay?'

'Not at all, and I am certainly not, but there was a gay element.'

'Tell us about this gay element, Mr Murray.'

'One day I was propositioned by a person named Sean Farrelly.'

'What exactly do you mean by propositioned?'

'He asked me to commit an indecent act with him, which I totally refused. I was then falsely accused of this act and subsequently charged.'

'You were charged? What was the outcome of this charge?'

'I was falsely convicted of this charge on the evidence of Michael Flanders and Sean Farrelly.'

'But then, was there not a turn in events and you were acquitted?'

'Yes, the accuser Sean Farrelly, retracted his statement and said he wanted forgiveness.'

'Why was that?'

'Because he was dying of the AIDS virus and he wanted forgiveness for the lie, so he could go to his grave in peace with his maker.'

'So, you forgave him?' Dermott felt his hand involuntarily touch his forehead as if to wipe away his perspiration. But to those with a more trained eye, it was to cover up the next lie he was about to tell. And he remembered something he had been taught at school about body language. Be careful to cover your tracks, because your body language never lies.

'I forgave him even though I had spent 12 months in a psychiatric prison. I joined the seminary to give myself to God and forgiveness is the whole essence of God's teaching.'

'Did you also forgive Michael Flanders, as well?'

'Of course, forgiveness is a natural part of wanting to be a priest.'

'So, you have no motive for wanting to poison Michael Flanders?'

'Of course not.'

'And you harbour no ill feeling toward him?'

'None at all. He has a far worse cross to bear than hatred from me.'

'Now Mr Murray, would you tell us how you came to be treating Mr Flanders with this new cure for AIDS?'

'I have been involved with the treatment of AIDS patients for a number of years now. It was my background in chemistry and biology that first brought me into this field. A list of volunteer patients came through to us and we took it from there.'

'You refer to the term us. Who else had access to the list of volunteers?'

'My colleague, Bradstreet, and the representatives from the Medical Council.'

'How were the prescriptions administered to the volunteers?'

'Under the strictest supervision, with a representative from the BMC always in attendance.'

'So, there was no way that the prescriptions could have been interfered in any way whatsoever.'

'Absolute impossibility, and in any case, I am committed to helping to save lives not destroying them.'

'I have finished, your honour, and thank you, Mr Murray.'

'Next witness.'

'Your honour, I wish to call Mr Bradstreet.'

'Fine, please proceed.'

'Mr Bradstreet, you work at the University of Liverpool and you have been a senior assistant to the accused Mr Dermott Murray for a number of years.'

'Yes.'

'Would you tell us a little more about Mr Murray. What sort of person is he? What he is like to work with?'

'I have worked with Dermott for about three years. During that time, I have found him to be honest, hardworking and totally reliable, and a person of the utmost integrity. Without him, we would not have made the inroads against this terrible AIDS virus.'

'He is a leading authority on the subject, is he not?'

'Yes, he is.'

'Mr Bradstreet, we have heard that you assisted with the preparation of the prescriptions for the AIDS trialists.'

'That is correct.'

'Tell me, is there any way in your opinion, that the capsules, I think that is the correct way of describing them, could have been tampered with by anyone, including Mr Murray?'

'None whatsoever. All the capsules were made up under strict supervision. You would also need to be a genius in every aspect of medicine. It would be too difficult and complicated.'

'Even for an expert like Mr Murray?'

'Yes, even for Dermott Murray.'

'Mr Bradstreet, would you say from your knowledge of Dermott Murray that he would be capable of poisoning anyone?'

'No, he is too caring a person.'

'Thank you, Mr Bradstreet, no further questions. Your honour, I wish to call my final witness, Dr Rose, from the Northern crime squad.' Rose a tall athletic specimen entered the box.

'Dr Rose, would you please tell members of the jury your qualifications and background.'

'I am Dr David Rose, forensic scientist and I work for the Northern crime squad based in Preston, Lancashire.'

'Dr Rose, how did you become involved with this case?'

'It is normal practice to call in someone, such as myself, in crimes of a serious nature. My role was to ensure that all necessary forensic tests were carried out in connection with this case. This involved the workplace of the accused, the equipment he used and also several searches and tests at his home in Ireland. Generally speaking, we examined anything that might yield a clue to evidence of poisoning.'

'The tests were very thorough then?'

'Most certainly.'

'Did you find anything?'

'To date, we have found nothing.'

'Would that indicate that my client is innocent then?'

'Objection, your honour,' interrupted Cusack.

'Objection sustained. Do not lead the witness, Mr Mowbray.'

'I apologise, your honour, that was not my intention.'

'Please answer, as you feel fit Dr Rose.'

'It means that we have found no evidence to date.'

'Dr Rose do all laboratories by their very nature hold poisons?'

'Yes, most of them do.'

'Does that normally include hemlock?'

'Not in all cases, but in this case, yes.'

'This hemlock, did you find anything untoward about it?'

'It had been disturbed, but that could have been someone moving the substance around and in most laboratories this happens all the time. Therefore, we did not think there was anything suspicious about that.'

'Examination complete, your honour.'

Flanders entered the box once more as Mowbray shuffled some papers. There was a brief pause, which seemed like an eternity to Flanders.

'Mr Flanders, I wonder if I may ask you a personal question?' The way Mowbray delivered his question was meant to disarm Flanders and when the question came it did.

'Would you say you are an animal lover?' Flanders had not

expected such nasty attack and he attacked back.

'Yes, why wouldn't I be an animal lover?'

'It's just that if you knew your prescription was poisoned, why on earth would you wish to inflict a slow death to a poor defenceless creature that could do nothing to defend itself?'

'I had no other choice.'

'Could you have not taken your prescription direct to the analyst instead of harming the creature?'

'I just wanted to be sure.'

'But we have heard the evidence and it appears that there is grave doubt that your cat died from any form of poisoning. The procedures used by Dr Taylor and his team very likely point to some form of *accidental* poisoning from the faulty hypodermic syringe. Indeed for all we know it still could have died from natural causes. Dr Wright indicated as much. What do you have to say to that?'

'I know nothing about poisons, which is why I went to the experts.'

'So, by your own admission, you no nothing about poisons?'

'Yes, I have told you so.'

'Then I ask you, why did you think your cat had been poisoned?'

'Because of what happened to Patrick Mahoney.' The judge interrupted quite severely.

'Mr Flanders *you* will answer questions relating to your own case. You will not assume anything in relation to the late Patrick Mahoney. The facts relating to Patrick Mahoney are not central to this case. Do you understand?'

'Yes, your honour.'

'One final question, Mr Flanders. We have heard from Dr Wright, who informs us that he too, found a similar substance to hemlock during an autopsy and he, too, was using the same type of hypodermic needle that a government department has outlawed, as seriously faulty. I ask you, therefore, is there not a shadow of doubt over the whole issue of your cat having been poisoned?'

'Well, obviously it appears that some of the syringes may be flawed.'

'But my question to you is this. Do you still believe that Mr Murray deliberately tried to taint your medication?'

The room went silent for a second or two in anticipation, everyone unsure, as to what his actual answer would be.

Flanders paused and then delivered his reply.

'In my opinion, Dermott Murray is a poisoner and he deliberately tried to poison me in revenge for me giving evidence against him.'

'No further questions, Mr Flanders.'

The session was finished for the day and reconvened next morning when Mowbray called his final witness.

'Your honour, I wish to call Mr Douglas Friedman who is the vice president of the Pioneering Medical Technology Company, USA.'

'Mr Friedman, you are the Vice President of the Pioneering Medical Technology Company?'

'Yes sir, I am,' he answered in a long Texan drawl.

'How long have you been in this position, Mr Friedman?'

'For seven years now, sir.'

'Is it fair to say your company has been the leading light in medical enhancement?'

'Yes sir, our company has developed many new technologies over the years for the benefit of the medical profession worldwide. I would go as far as to say we are the leaders in this field and we intend to stay so.'

'Your company has enjoyed considerable success and has an enviable reputation.'

'That is about the top and bottom of it.'

'Does you company have a budget for development and research?'

'Ten million dollars last year, sir.'

'Is that a small sum or a large sum compared to your competitors?'

'Just about the largest in the States at this present time.'

'Mr Friedman, your company developed a new hypodermic syringe about 18 months ago, one which helps to prevent the spread of AIDS.'

'A major breakthrough of its kind.'

'Did you not have some problems in recent times with the reliability of this instrument?'

'No sir, it was not the instrument itself, it was the components that the actual needle is constructed of. You see, it is constructed from malleable plastic and nylon and in some cases when this came into contact with body fluid, a poisonous substance could be discharged into the bloodstream.'

'Was this likely to happen often?' Friedman didn't wish to

answer this question, as it would reflect badly on his company's reputation.

'No sir. But once we knew about this malfunction, all production ceased as a temporary measure. We have almost solved the problem now.'

'Mr Friedman, how many times, say out of a hundred, was this likely to happen?' He was becoming uncomfortable and he didn't know how to answer. After all, he was used to American law and not an English court.

'I am not sure we have any definite statistics but I am sure it couldn't be more than ten out of a hundred. So shall we say about 10%?'

'This poisonous substance, could it be life threatening?'

'Well I guess so, that is why we stopped production.'

'So, your company which is a multi-million conglomerate has been honest enough to admit, that despite being highly successful and respected, it cannot always get it right?'

'Yes, we need to be honest with little old Joe public.'

'Mr Friedman, I thank you most sincerely for giving your evidence today. I have no further questions, your honour.'

Patrick Cusack, in his closing speech for the prosecution, dealt first with the evidence of the witnesses. He then proceeded with his summary.

'Members of the jury, we have all heard the evidence regarding the poisonous substance that caused the death of the cat belonging to Mr Flanders. It is apparent to me that it was impossible for the animal to have consumed or inhaled this substance in any normal way. Dr Taylor said as much. Therefore, surely, the only logical conclusion you could possibly come to, is that Dermott Murray administered the hemlock with the sole intent of harming Mr Flanders. If you think carefully about this, first of all, he had the motive.' Cusack paused deliberately so as to add more effect to the next part of his statement.

'Secondly, and just as importantly, he was an expert in dealing with poisonous substances. And lastly, ladies and gentlemen, he had the opportunity to tamper with the capsules. What more evidence do you need? I am sure you will come to the right conclusion.'

It was then the turn of Mowbray to finalise.

'Members of the jury, there is very little for me to say, save that you have heard from many witnesses. I am sure you are all sensible people. Dr Taylor freely admits that his department used a process that had been outlawed by the authorities as being unreliable. Dr Wright says that there was a lack of the poison in the very areas in which you would expect to find it. That is the spleen, the liver and the tissues. What more explanation is required. Finally, you have heard the testimony from my client. Here is a Christian man a caring, forgiving man. Why else would he have studied for the priesthood? You heard him say he had forgiven his enemies. He also refers to the fact that Mr Flanders has a far worse cross to bear from the disease, than from himself. I need elaborate no further, my client cannot be possibly guilty of these charges.'

The case had been going on for nine days and now it was the turn of the judge to sum up.

'What I have to say in my summing up will take quite some time. This court will adjourn until Tuesday morning.'

Chapter Thirty

It was the third week in November and a thick fog had drifted in from the Mersey and hardly moved for two days. This was accompanied by a dank smell pervading the city buildings, which was a combination of traffic fumes and pollution from a nearby chemical factory on the Bootle Road. It all added to a gloomy atmosphere, but that did not prevent public interest in the case from reaching new heights. There was standing room only in the public gallery. The judge was in ebullient form as he commenced his summing up.

'Members of the jury, having heard both sets of evidence, the first thing you have to determine is whether the dead animal met its death by poison or not. If so, had the poison been administered by the accused? The learned counsel for the accused had endeavoured to show that there was no real motive for this crime, because Mr Murray a caring man, had forgiven his enemies and had stated that Mr Flanders was suffering enough, from the AIDS virus itself. Should the treatment for the virus not be successful, then it is a possibility that Mr Flanders might not survive anyway,' and he uttered the last few words in as sympathetic a tone as he could manage.

'Even with the remarkable progress that has been made against this virus, the odds are certainly not in favour of Mr Flanders. Anyone suffering with this particular strain of virus still only has a seven percent chance of survival. I cannot remind you all enough however, not take this factor as an isolated factor, but as one of a number of distinguishing factors in connection with this case. It is your job to decide whether there is a real motive for this crime. It is also a fact in favour of the accused that no evidence has been found to suggest he actually tampered with the hemlock contained in the laboratory. There is no proof that the capsules were tainted and none of the poison was found at his home during or after the time of his arrest. You must also remember that the poor unfortunate animal may have died a natural death from the result of dysentery.

You must be guided by those rules of common sense, that operate on the minds of reasonable people and even if there were no medical testimony, you still have a very grave decision to decide to the guilt or innocence of the accused. Foreman for the jury, would you please retire to consider your verdict?'

Dermott retired with his counsel to discuss some minor points. Once more, the balance of his future was in the hands of 12 complete strangers.

Chapter Thirty One

The popular press having committed itself deeply to supporting Michael Flanders, because it would sell more newspapers, had to make the best of the next few days, suggesting that because the jury were taking so long in their deliberation, it was inevitable the final outcome would be GUILTY. Five days elapsed and still there was no verdict. The judge reminded the jury that he would accept a majority verdict if necessary and he was about to issue further dialogue to the jury, when Flanders' counsel disturbed him.

'Your honour, we request an *immediate* hearing with yourself and the counsel for the accused, on a matter of extreme importance, so important, that it may well have an effect on the case we are all dealing with.'

'Very well, my chambers at 4pm. May I add, it had better be *important.*'

Cusack sat in front of the judge looking rather agitated and yet smug at the same time. He commenced slowly but then started to gabble and realised he might be overstepping the mark.

'Your honour, we have evidence linking Dermott Murray to the death of Patrick Mahoney!'

'The judge was taken aback; he had not expected *this* evidence. 'From the exhumation?'

'Actually, no. The remains were too badly de-composed.'

'You had better bring in Dr Rose then.'

A measured step was heard upon the stairs. A moment later, the tall, stout, solemnly respectable, Dr Rose was ushered into the room.

'Good afternoon, Dr Rose, you have something of vital importance to impart to us? What form does this evidence take?'

'Your honour, the Northern crime squad felt no stone should be left unturned, even though it is a fair time since Patrick Mahoney passed away. A search was made of the old property he last lived in. It has new owners now of course, so a search warrant was obtained and a member of the team sent down to Devon. It was there that we had an unexpected piece of luck. The new owners have let the place become a bit dilapidated and we had a fair job on our hands. Rubbish and bits of junk lying around in the back garden. In the greenhouse were lots of dirty plant pots, some full of potting compost and one or two with roots growing out, or in some cases, dying in the pots. Next to one of the pots, we found the corpse of a dead squirrel. Nothing strange in that, you may ask. But next to the squirrel were the remains of two dead birds. The forensic team took a few samples from this pot analysis. And low and behold, what did we come up with? A substance similar to *coniine* or hemlock! As we were confused about the corpses, we contacted Pest Control and they gave us a simple explanation. Squirrels have a habit of burying walnuts while they are still green in the hope of finding them at a later date. If left untouched in potting compost, these eventually split and form shoots of their own.

Pest Control inform us, it is most likely the squirrel returned for its tasty snack and if the compost was contaminated with this *coniine*, then it is almost certain that the creature died from hemlock poison. The birds had probably pecked the dead animal and become infected themselves.'

'One wonders why the *coniine* came to be in the pot?'

'Minute traces somehow placed in there by the deceased......... and the odds of this deadly substance being found by pure chance?'

'Too staggering to contemplate.'

'Therefore, Dr Rose it looks as if you have your man.'

The judge extracted an old thick volume from an oak-panelled built in bookcase. Looking through the index he found the name he was searching for – Joseph Petts and then turned to the chapter for the historic case notes. It was Friday. On the Tuesday following, the jury was re-called to his chambers.

'Members of the jury, have you yet reached a verdict?' The foreman replied. 'No, your honour, we are still deliberating.'

'It is a difficult case, I admit that. Anyhow, it is my duty to inform you that you will be hearing new evidence shortly, in connection with the suspected poisoning of the late Patrick Mahoney. Charges are being brought against the accused, Dermott Murray, in connection with this. In the meantime, I am *suspending* the case of Michael Flanders versus Dermott Murray. You are discharged of your *present* duties forthwith. But you will be sworn in later this week to hear the case of the late Patrick Mahoney. You must not discuss the case of Michael Flanders with anyone, not even amongst yourselves, even though there is a connection between the two cases. You *will* be allowed, however, *to take into account* the evidence you have heard with regard to the case of Michael Flanders, inasmuch that some of it will be relevant in the new case of the late Patrick Mahoney. This is a point of law. But I must reiterate to you all, that the two cases remain separate. Is this clear to you all? May I add that I have checked my facts thoroughly via case history and it is quite in order for me to take this course of action.' The tabloid press was having a field day at the expense of Dermott who was having difficulty in concealing his agitated step and trembling countenance.

'Dermott, why has this trouble, misery and persecution been heaped upon us? Look at us. We are now unfortunate wretches, who cannot even see from where these afflictions come from. If I did not know better, I would say we have been in contact with the devil himself, so much bad luck has befallen us.' Each word fell like a dagger and deprived him of his energy. Dermott looked around him and raised his eyes towards the ceiling, but withdrew them immediately, as if he feared the roof might open and reveal a tribunal called heaven and a judge named God. Both his confidence and *his* God seemed to be deserting him. Teresa's comments were too near to the knuckle for his liking.

'Teresa, if it is that serious, why do the police let me out to see you?'

'Probably because there is a lot of public sentiment. After all, you are the pioneer, the possible saviour of some poor devils who cannot help themselves. Remember you are considered the expert in your field.'

'Once this absurd case is out of the way perhaps we can move forward….. make a fresh start.'

'A fresh start? A good start would be for you to visit the hospital as you promised. Just look at the child we have brought into the world. A quivering wreck. God is punishing us; there is no other explanation for it.'

'I was overtaken by the trial.'

'Yes and now one trial has been suspended, you now have another to face. When is it all going to end, will there be *another* case after this?'

In an attempt to sell more newspapers, the press started to take the side the side of Dermott. 'How can AIDS pioneer be a poisoner?' read one such headline. Dermott mistakenly read this as support for his cause and did not realise he was following a false path.

And now for the second time in as many months, the jurors were once more listening to evidence very similar to that in the case of Michael Flanders. Only this time, they had to be convinced that Dermott had tried to poison Patrick Mahoney. Cusack once more commenced his verbal attack on Dermott.

'Mr Murray, I put it to you, that in retribution for Patrick Mahoney giving evidence against you, you then sought your revenge, by trying to poison him. Not only did you have a motive, but you also had the means at your disposal.' Dermott started acting again and then looking Cusack directly in the eye, he replied.

'I have already told you, my job is to save lives, not destroy them.'

'Yes, we have heard that before, Mr Murray. But how do you account for the *coniine* being found at Mr Mahoney's property. Secondly, is it not too much of a coincidence that the cat belonging to Mr Flanders also had the very same substance in its system? I would suggest that you deliberately tainted the medication of both Mr Mahoney and then Mr Flanders. Is that not the case?'

The judge interrupted once more. 'Mr Cusack, would you please stick to the subject matter, which is the case of the late Patrick Mahoney. We are not dealing with the case of Mr Flanders.'

'Apologies, your honour. Mr Murray, I ask you once more, did you taint the medication of Patrick Mahoney?'

'No, that is not the case. The poison must have found its way there by other means.' Dermott was beginning to lose his nerve and his thought process.

'Ah, so now you are saying the poison did exist?'

'I am not saying that. I am saying if the medication became tainted, it must have been during the packaging.'

'But you told us that the packaging was conducted under the strictest supervision.'

'That is correct.'

'Mr Murray, I am not really sure you know what you are saying and from the sound of it, I don't think you know what you are saying. I think you are trying to conceal the truth from the jury. Mr Murray, if the prescription was contaminated by accident, why were not the others in the same batch contaminated? Mr Murray, I do not think you are coming clean with us. The evidence is pretty strong and I suggest that you deliberately tainted the prescription to seek your own retribution.'

'That is just not true, all medication was made up under strict supervision.'

'No more questions, your honour.'

Carruthers took the stand. A tall, bony individual with lean features and a dark complexion.

'Your honour and members of the jury, this is Mr Paul Carruthers from the tropical school of medicine. Mr Carruthers you are the senior lecturer at the Tropical School of Medicine, are you not?'

'I am indeed.'

'Before that, I understand you worked on both the African and European continents, researching and developing antidotes for some of the most deadly poisons on the planet.'

'Yes, I did.'

'Would you please tell us what you know about the substance hemlock or *coniine* as it is sometimes referred to?'

'The substance comes from a European plant of the parsley family. The poison, an oily liquid, is made from the plant. The bark is sometimes used in the tanning process.'

'Mr Carruthers, would you say that this substance is likely to be found in a back garden?'

'Absolutely not. For this substance to be found in any form, it would have to have been placed there by someone who knows about poisons.'

'Someone who deals with them on a regular basis then.'

'Objection, your honour, the witness is being lead.'

'Objection overruled.'

'So the chances of it being found in a domestic property in the UK are most unlikely?'

'Yes, unless someone was involved in tanning, but all tanning should take place on commercial property anyway.'

'Mr Carruthers, what would you say the odds are of finding this substance in my garden or your garden say.'

'The odds are millions to one against.'

'Unless someone actually had access to this substance and a motive for dabbling with it. Would that be a fair comment?'

'Yes, that is about right.'

'This someone would need to be an expert in this field, would he not?'

'Oh, without a doubt.'

'Now if someone were to inhale or consume this substance, what would be the likely outcome?'

'Death would result very quickly.'

'I see, and the symptoms associated with this might be?'

'Eventually the lungs would fail or the heart become paralysed.'

'Would there be any post mortem signs?'

'There would be hardly any signs at all save for those associated with asphyxia.'

'Thank you, Mr Carruthers, that is all. Your honour, I wish to call Dr Spencer coroner involved for the late Patrick Mahoney. Dr Spencer, you are a coroner are you not and you carried out the post mortem on the late Patrick Mahoney?'

'Yes that is correct.'

'Dr Spencer, would you please tell the members of the jury what, in your opinion, was the cause of Patrick Mahoney's death?'

'The actual cause of death, as I stated in my report, was asphyxia.'

'Please tell us, in simple terms, what this medical term means.'

'In medical terms, it actually means a loss of consciousness as a result of too little oxygen and too much carbon dioxide in the blood. This is commonly referred to as suffocation or being unable to breath. In Patrick Mahoney's case, he actually drowned.'

'Did you find anything abnormal during your examination?'

'No, I did not but the body had been in the sea for some time and this coupled with the fact that he was dying from the AIDS virus would have merely disguised any abnormalities.'

'Would it be possible to have inadvertently taken this substance and subsequently died from it with no apparent symptoms other than asphyxia?'

'Well I suppose that is possible, but as I say, it would have been impossible to tell because of the suffocation in the water and the AIDS virus weakening the body generally.' Cusack allowed himself to smile but it was a bitter sarcastic smile that came to his lips.

'Would you not agree a pretty good cover for hemlock poisoning?'

'Well, yes, as I have said it could be possible but………..'

Thank you Dr Spencer, that is all for now.' Mowbray was next to his feet. It appeared that Dermott's case had weakened rather rapidly, especially after the evidence given by both, Carruthers and Spencer. The word from the courtroom indicated that he was swimming against the tide. To make it all worse, Mowbray was running short on ammunition with which to defend Dermott and once more Cusack seemed to have all the aces in the pack.

'Your honour, I also would like to call Dr Spencer to the stand.'

'That is in order.'

'Dr Spencer we have heard your evidence a few minutes ago which was very illuminating. May I ask you how long you have been qualified as a coroner?'

'19 years.'

'19 years, a very long time indeed, which I would say, makes you very experienced at your chosen profession. During that time, have you come across other cases such as the one we are dealing with?'

'I can't recall that I have.'

'Now, we noted that you stated death was caused by drowning, which we all understand was a correct diagnosis. No one is questioning your abilities at all. However, I would just like to check something with you. Had the case of the late Patrick Mahoney simply passed into the historic files like so many others, would you have ever had cause to, or occasion, to consider that your first diagnosis had been incorrect?'

'No reason whatsoever, there was no evidence to suspect anything untoward at the time, only possibly in retrospect.'

'No more questions Dr Spencer, thank you.'

'Your honour, I call Mr Gerrard Fellows.'

Fellows was well groomed and trimly clad with something of refinement in his bearing.

'Mr Fellows, you are a coroner and specialist for her majesty's government dealing in the gruesome business of exhumation, are you not?'

'I am indeed.'

'Please inform us what sort of cases you are involved in.'

'I oversee the most serious cases those rated as 'Category A' by the crime squad. That generally means where foul play or suspected murder *may* have taken place.'

'That is why you were called upon to investigate this case of the late Mr Mahoney.'

'It is indeed.'

'So, after the body of Mr Mahoney had been exhumed, did you find anything to suggest that death was from anything other then natural causes?'

'The chances of us finding anything at all, after all the time that had elapsed, were so remote so as to render the task nigh on impossible. And we did not find anything. It looked as if death had occurred from drowning as indicated in the report by Dr Spencer. Even with the progress in modern science, our chances of finding anything were slim at the very best.'

'I have no further questions and thank you, Mr Fellows.'

Mowbray was getting worried. He wanted to leave a good impression on the jury before they retired and that time was getting closer.

Dermott was called.

'Mr Murray, please tell us the very strict procedures for making up the prescriptions for the AIDS trialists.'

'The components have to be prepared three days in advance of final distribution. The elements that make up the final capsule are mashed into a paste and left for 48 hours. 24 hours before completion, a further component is added, and then this new mixture is left to freeze and eventually dried off in a special ventilator.'

'Who actually prepares the components?'

'My assistant, Mr Bradstreet and myself. All this is done under the watchful eye of a representative from the British Medical Council.'

'I see, so at no time are you and Mr Bradstreet ever left unsupervised?' Dermott hesitated as the lie was about to come, but then he coughed so as to deflect away from the lie.

'Absolutely correct.'

'There is no way, therefore, that you could have interfered with the prescriptions?'

'None whatsoever.'

'Mr Murray, would you still say that you are a man of God?' Beads of sweat began to form under Dermott's armpits and he could feel a prickly sensation on his forehead. He knew he would have to lie in the most dramatic fashion he could muster. He did have a God but not the God that Mowbray alluded to.

'Although I did not eventually stay in the priesthood, I have never ceased being a man of God.'

'Mr Murray, what, in your opinion, is the noblest character trait that we as human beings possess?'

'Without a doubt, it is to love thy neighbour as thyself. This was at the very core of the teachings of Jesus. I still have no reason to think otherwise.'

'So, to cause harm to ones fellow man is not in your nature?'

'It is totally alien to my nature.'

'Mr Murray, out of all the AIDS trialists, would you say some have a better chance of survival than others?'

'Without a doubt, some have a better physiological make up than others. In some cases the virus is more advanced than others.'

'In the case of the late Patrick Mahoney then, would you say he had a better chance of survival than others?' Dermott had been hoping for a question along these lines.

'I would say that he had a slightly worse chance than the others.'

'Why would that be?'

'Because the virus had attacked his nervous system making him more susceptible to other infectious agents.'

'One final matter, Mr Murray. If you could turn back the clock, would you have still entered the seminary?'

'Quite definitely. I wanted to join the priesthood, it is just that the almighty wanted me for another purpose, which was to help heal the sick.'

'Nothing further to ask, Mr Murray.'

For the second time, Dermott's assistant, Bradstreet, was about to be cross-examined by Mowbray.

'Mr Bradstreet, we have earlier heard the glowing reference you gave Mr Murray. I just want the members of the jury to be absolutely certain over the matter relating to the preparing of the prescriptions. Can you, with absolute certainty be sure that the capsules were not tainted with any poisonous substance?'

'Totally impossible for the capsules to become contaminated.'

'At no time, therefore, could the accused, your friend and your colleague, have been left on his own to interfere with the capsules?'

'I cannot recall such a time. Mr Bentley from the BMC was late one day, but Mr Murray and I waited until he arrived, before we commenced the work.'

'Remember, you are on oath and you are telling me that on no occasion was Mr Murray left on his own?'

Dermott dropped his head to look at the floor, in order to avoid a blush that began to spread across his face. 'My God he thought; I hope you give the correct answer Bradstreet.'

Bradstreet paused as if trying to recall an event that would surely be damning for Dermott. At last he spoke.

'Mr Murray did occasionally work on his own.' A hubbub of noise broke out across the courtroom.

'Silence in my court,' once more roared the judge.

'Mr Bradstreet, continue.'

Bradstreet continued slowly as if he had just been awoken from a dream.

'But that was before we commenced preparing the vaccines.' The courtroom went silent again and the audience watching this spectacle, sighed as if they had just been relieved from a great stress that had been weighing them down. And now there was an anti-climax as Bradstreet added.

'Mr Murray was never left on his own while the vaccines were prepared. Of that fact, I am absolutely certain.'

'That is all, Mr Bradsteet, thank you.'

'Your honour I now wish to call Dr Sanderson. Dr Sanderson, you are one of the two BMC representatives that oversaw the preparation of the medication for the AIDS trialists, are you not?'

'I am indeed.'

'Dr Sanderson, we learnt from Mr Murray about the way the prescriptions were prepared. Would it have been possible for anyone to have interfered with the prescriptions in any way, so as to make them a deadly cocktail of poison?'

'Not in my opinion. There was always a representative from the Medical Council in attendance. This was my colleague, Mr Bentley, or myself. The components making up the medication were very delicate substances. If they were tampered with, the person doing this would have to be a very accomplished schemer, illusionist and a master at the art of deception. We were never allowed to leave the room while the process was being undertaken. Our professional careers would be at stake if we dared to do so.'

'So, you can assure the members of the jury that the capsules were free of any interference?'

'Without doubt.'

'Dr Sanderson although this session was very brief, you have been of great help, thank you.' All the witnesses had now been called and once again, it was time for Cusack to deliver his closing speech. He wanted desperately to deliver an *effect* on his audience but he found it difficult to bring about that effect, as the witnesses, evidence and nature of the crimes were so similar. Now his job, reputation and personal pride were all at risk and he would have to find a weakness in the armoury of Dermott Murray. He believed he had found one.

'Members of the jury, I am sure I don't need to remind you, that you are here to decide if Dermott Murray is guilty of the poisoning and murder of Patrick Mahoney. However, his honour has informed you, that you may take into account, when considering that verdict, the evidence also presented to you in the case of Michael Flanders. I implore you, therefore, not to forget that evidence, as there is a connection with the two cases. But once more, let us turn to the case in hand. What do we know? We know that the accused had a motive. A very strong motive. We know he was very accomplished in dealing with poisonous substances and we know he had the opportunity to tamper with the medication of Patrick Mahoney. Strong evidence would you not say, against the accused. And let me remind you of the testimony of Mr Carruthers'. He stated under oath that the odds of finding this poison *coniine* at any domestic property were millions to one against. Have you or are you ever likely to find this substance in your own back garden? I think not!' And Cusack delivered his words with such dramatic effect that his audience was spellbound. Dermott's case was weakening by the second. Mowbray stiffened. He knew, inwardly, that this was the most difficult case he had had to fight. He feared he was losing both the battle and the war. Mowbray commenced.

'Members of the jury. We have heard from many eminent witnesses. Experts in their field and they inform us that Patrick Mahoney died from asphyxia as a result of drowning. None of the experts can categorically confirm that the cause of death was from poisoning. And on top of that, the chances of him surviving very much longer were thin. He had, as we have heard, only a seven percent chance of survival. He was dying of AIDS.

You have also heard that my client is a God fearing man who was training to be a priest. Here is a man who is trying to save the lives, of those, whose chance of survival is very slim. You have seen him give evidence. Does he strike you as a callous cold, evil doer, or a person radiating warmth and respect for his fellow man? I am sure you will have no difficulty in reaching the correct decision.'

Chapter Thirty Two

And now, once more, it was time for the judge to sum up the case. He was no longer as impartial as he had been several weeks earlier, because the case was grating on his nervous system. Having been on the circuit many years, he had presided over many nasty cases and sentenced many evildoers to incarceration. Secretly he was not the impartial well-balanced individual he enacted. He was in reality a hard liner; intolerant specimen who made snap judgements in cases even *remotely* connected to homosexuality. He loathed any one who was involved with homosexuals and tarred them all with the same brush whether they be of normal persuasion or otherwise. His mistaken prejudice was that if you came in to contact with that caste, then you must be one of them! This did not bode well for Dermott. Once more he delved very fully into the evidence given in the case, but making particular reference to negative points against Dermott rather than the positive points in favour of his case.

'Members of the jury, a portion of the evidence went to show that the deceased died from natural causes, if drowning can be called a natural cause. But Dr Spencer stated that this could actually have disguised any form of poisoning and also remember that if *coniine* were the cause of death, there would have been no symptoms save those found with asphyxia.

The accused, ladies and gentlemen, had not only the motive for this crime, but the knowledge of dangerous substances and quite possibly, the opportunity to interfere with the medication. We have also learned that the chances of you or I coming across the deadly poison in our own back garden are too remote to even contemplate. Millions to one against so you have to ask yourself, how did this poison come to be found in the garden of Patrick Mahoney? Someone must have placed it there. If it wasn't actually placed there by Dermott Murray, ask yourself then, was there a connection between the deceased and Dermott Murray? We all know the answer to that. It would seem to me, that there are many factors and a few too many coincidences linking the accused with the death of Patrick Mahoney. On top of that, you need to remind yourself of the link between Dermott Murray and Michael Flanders, but please remember, you are here, to judge whether *Dermott Murray is guilty of poisoning Patrick Mahoney.* It is my opinion that you will not have difficulty in reaching a verdict in *this* case.' Dermott was already preparing himself for defeat but with every word that came from the judge, he felt weaker and weaker. It felt as though a hoard of termites were burrowing into his flesh and slowly sucking his lifeblood. Once the judge had uttered the words 'You will not have difficulty in reaching a verdict' he became pale and agitated and as he reached for a tumbler of water, Mowbray whispered 'Are you all right?' He replied hoarsely, 'Yes, I am ok.'

The press were gripped by the sensationally of the case. It helped them sell newspapers. Now it was the turn of the judge to come under fire. Several of the papers commented on the conduct of the man. In various parts of the trial and especially in the summing up, his conduct was rather that of an advocate for the prosecution than that of the occupant of the bench holding fairly the trembling balance of justice. He did not seem to remember that the liberty of a man was at stake. The Times took particular dislike to Taylor, the Chief Public Analyst.

'This man who par excellence was looked upon as the pillar of medical jurisprudence; the man who it was believed could clear up the most obscure case, involving medico-legal considerations, ever brought into a court of justice, the man whose opinion could be relied upon in every case, is the same man who has now admitted, he used equipment that was outlawed by the government. We must now look upon Dr Taylor as having ended his career and hope he will immediately withdraw into the obscurity of private life, not forgetting to carry with him his hypodermic syringe.'

The Telegraph commented generally of the debacle.

'This farce must no longer be exhibited to the world, of the most celebrated toxicologists contradicting each other in matters where there should be no possibility of doubt. The liberty of a man is at stake; this is not a case of one expert trying to score points over another.'

The tabloids were more in keeping with their normal type of storytelling and were rather more forceful and direct. One of the gutter press thus summed up its views:

'Is Dermott Murray guilty? – We believe he is

Has he been proved guilty? - Certainly not

The balance of probabilities is against him, but there is a

possibility that he may be innocent. Innocent men have been found guilty on circumstantial evidence as strong as that in this case. The paper went on to refer to him as a calculating cold-hearted liar with both the motive and means to have carried out such an evil deed.

He was described as a scoundrel a cheat of the blackest dye in every walk of life. But without doubt it was felt that the charge of poison and attempted murder had not been satisfactorily proved. Whatever the verdict is to be if it is a just one or not only the Great Judge can show. If it can be shown and we think it can, the general public have a right to demand that the proofs of poisoning be so clear that no reasonable man can have a doubt about the matter. In almost every case of poisoning two things have been clearly proved. Poison has been found in unmistakable quantities in the body, or it has been traced to the possession the supposed poisoner. In this case, no poison could be definitely traced to the accused himself and poison was not found in the exhumed remains of Patrick Mahoney.' And so it went on in a frenzied manner each paper trying to out do another so much so that Dermott refused to read any of them. His stress level was at breaking point.

Three days, the jury had been deliberating and still no verdict. This case had all the hallmarks of being an epic.

Two more days elapsed, 120 hours and Dermott could hardly contain his anxiety. He supplicated his God to end this misery and release him back into society but still there was no redeeming call from the court. Nothing but the same mundane activities, from early morning until early evening. A weekend intervened another 48 hours for Dermott to wonder and worry about the verdict of the jury. Monday morning arrived to a grey dismal dank day. The judge recalled the jury and informed them he would accept a majority verdict.

'I cannot quite understand what is causing you to take so long?' he added as if to hurry them into a decision.

The foreman spoke at length to the rest of his audience.

'So for the umpteenth time, we are all agreed that he tried to poison Patrick Mahoney. To add weight to that argument, is the fact that the odds of *coniine* being found in a back garden are millions to one against.'

Several of the jury nodded in agreement. The foreman continued slowly.

'But we are all pretty sure that the prosecution did not actually prove the case for poisoning and there was no evidence of poisoning in Patrick Mahoney's remains. So where does that leave us?'

The small thin Irish women piped up again. 'I have told you before, a good Catholic lad studying for the priesthood could not have such terrible thoughts in his heart. They just do not think like that.'

The red-haired man, who had said very little up until now, spoke up.

'Absolute twaddle, how do you know that?'

'Because I have a nephew who is a priest. Those studying for the priesthood do not contemplate evil.' Someone nodded her agreement. Before the foreman could speak, she interjected once more.

'Let me ask you all. How many Catholics have we on this jury?'

Almost involuntarily, eight hands went up. The foreman was losing control as she continued.

'As good Catholics, ask yourself, if this was you, or your son, would you have contemplated such evil. Examine your conscience and ask yourself.' The room went strangely silent for a few seconds.

Now the red-haired man was becoming irritable 'I am not a Catholic and I don't have a son, and I think he is guilty.'

The red-haired man now received support from two other jurors as they nodded in agreement. The foreman tried to show some authority.

'We had better take a vote on this, but before we do, we need a brake. Let's return in 15 minutes.' Over drinks of refreshment, the jury dispersed into three groups of four either by design or by accident. Soon, however, one group merged into eight and this group appeared to be discussing the merits of the Catholic priesthood. Not noticing this had happened, the foreman was powerless to stop the convergence.

Suddenly, a group of three formed and from the conversation it was apparent that *this* group, was discussing the merits of the larger group. Feeling most uncomfortable, the foreman endeavoured to move all the jurors back into the consulting room, but now either both groups had not heard him or were totally ignoring him. The situation was becoming very awkward. The last thing he wished for was for prejudice to creep in. It was difficult enough to reach a decision without this added aggravation. At length the two factions dispersed but it was now apparent that two distinct groups had formed, because now the larger group was eyeing the smaller group with slight disdain. The foreman realised that this aggravation was now becoming a major burden. He was hoping against hope that this would not affect their consideration in reaching a verdict.

'Well, I hope we have cleared our heads and that we all remain impartial. Now have we reached any conclusion?' Now the Irish women wouldn't keep quiet.

'We have.'

'We?' asked the foreman. 'Exactly who are you referring to?'

'Our group here, and several nodded in agreement.

'Look, this is an individual matter, we cannot have groups.'

'Well, our group has made a decision.'

'For the second time, we cannot have groups. All decisions have to be impartial and independently arrived at.'

'Well, I have told you he cannot possibly be guilty, a good lad like that.'

The foreman looked at the rest of the jurors.

'I will ask you all in order. Now, next, what is your verdict?'

'I agree, not guilty.' The third person gave the same answer. By the time he reached the fourth, he almost knew what the answer would be.

'Not guilty.' He continued until the group was exhausted extracting eight not guilty verdicts. Now he knew it was game set and match. The last three gave their verdicts, all of which were guilty. The foreman was devastated as he spoke.

'My verdict is guilty, but I am more than concerned at how we reached our decisions. It seems to me that some of you feel that because this man was about to enter the priesthood, it somehow makes him innocent. In my book, that is no sane and reasonable way to arrive at a decision. Hadn't we better discuss this at length?'

Now, one of the other jurors spoke. She also was a supporter of the Irish woman. 'I am not changing my decision and I am not discussing this any further. How about the rest of you?' Immediately she obtained the support and same answer from her peers.

'We have been out too long by far and I have been convinced, now, that he his not guilty.' The foreman was at his wits end.

'So, we have eight not guilty verdicts and four guilty. Is that the final answer of you all?'

The red-haired man spoke once more.

'As far as I can see, he is as guilty as hell. He had the motive, the opportunity and the odds of finding that poison in a garden are millions to one against. Guilty, that is my final answer.' His counterparts all agreed.

'Well, I don't like the way we have reached the decision. It seems as if we have formed two separate groups since this business of the 'priesthood' came up. It seems like prejudice to me.'

'Prejudice or otherwise, we have reached our decisions.'

'Shall we think about it overnight?'

'If you wish, but nothing will change.' And with this, the jury departed and the foreman was somehow hoping the matter would resolve itself by the morning. He tried to imagine who might be swayed and who would not be swayed and by the time the morning had arrived he sensed an air of nonchalance around the room. One by one the jurors delivered their verdicts in a cold calculating manner and once more, Dermott would be free to weave his trail of misery.

The jury entered the chamber shuffling and scraping as they took to their places. The court took its seat and so did everybody else. There was a moment's silence, during which one could have fancied the hall empty, so profound was the stillness. The spectators' gallery was completely full and journalists abounded, pens at the ready. The judge entered, looking every bit as though he stood for the vindication of society. Today, he represented the law, the scales of justice, and on this last morning, there appeared nothing human about him. He looked as though he were enjoying the spectacle. This was not how he had portrayed himself earlier in the trial. It was as if he welcomed all the pairs of eyes gazing upon him as if *he* were the centre of attraction. He lowered the lids over his vulturish eyes and stared at the jury piercingly from his full height. He did not take off his robe and he leaned on his two great ham-sized hands. He lent over a little so as to dominate the jury and he looked as though he were saying 'You had better have come up with the right answer, for this little shit, this poofter, deserves all he gets. And as far as I am concerned, he should be locked up on his own and we should throw away the key. Now I want to hear the correct verdict and you know what that is.'

Dermott dressed modestly and tried to look calm and natural and put on his 'priestly demeanour' in the hope of once more subconsciously affecting the members of the jury, particularly the old ladies, into thinking he was a godly man. This was a ploy he had used throughout his trial. Secretly, however, he didn't harbour much hope. His game plan had been rumbled. The evidence, explaining that *coniine* would never be found in a back garden, had been a stunner. He had not and could not have accounted for this evidence having been presented, especially at two different addresses. But he promised himself he would not flinch when the verdict was read out.

At length, the judge spoke.
'Members of the jury, have you at last reached a verdict?'
'We have, your honour.'
'The verdict you have reached, is that of you all?'
'No, your honour, it is not.'
'Then you have a majority verdict?'
'Yes, we do.'
'Then foreman, please tell us what is your verdict?'
A tension gripped the room as the audience prepared for the reply.
'By a majority of eight to four, we find the accused not guilty!' Pandemonium broke out and cheer upon cheer rent the roof. The judge looked at the foreman with a look of disbelief and then he felt his anger rise. His cheeks puffed out. He was angry both at the verdict and the noise in his court. Dermott had a look of incredulity on his face, which he tried to remove instantaneously.
'If this noise does not cease, I shall dismiss you all, except those who are duty bound to stay.'
The chief usher spoke up in a rather loud manner. 'Silence in court. We must have silence!'
'You are telling me your verdict is not guilty by a majority of eight to four?'
'That is correct, your honour.' Now there was anger and a hint of bitterness in his voice. The following day the press were to make a meal of his next comments in a headline banner, such was the sarcastic tone, with which he delivered the words.
'Well, obviously the accused is free and this court is closed.' Hoards of well wishers seemed to appear from nowhere and Dermott was being slapped on the back. There were noises and comments in the background, which he heard but did not seem to take in. 'Well done, Dermott, I knew in my heart you were not guilty.'

The press and television cameras were at the ready and a microphone thrust under his chin.

'Have you any comments Dermott? Did you think you would get off?'

Dermott tried to remain calm.

'I only have this to say. I knew that I was not guilty and put my trust in my God and today I have been justly repaid.' That will do for all the media, he thought to himself and he tried to walk away from the hubbub and flashbulbs that had invaded his world. Back in the courtroom, there was a look of amazement on the face of two people who had merely been witnesses since the day of Dermott's arrest. They had played little part in the case since then, merely being cogs in the wheel. Their job had been to compile the case and get it into court. Since that time, they had merely watched the drama unfold and Dermott had almost forgotten them, so overwhelmed and consumed had he been by the constant questioning by all sorts of people, especially the barristers and witnesses that had been brought to bear.

'Bill, I cannot fathom how this bloody jury have arrived at such a decision. It is absolute nonsense. What went wrong? We have heard the evidence regarding the *coniine*. The odds are millions to one against the stuff being found in a bloody back garden. Are they all mad? He is as guilty as hell.'

'Well, I know that and you know that, but we are stuffed, the bastard has got off.'

'Not just once, but bloody twice.'

'I know, that makes it twice as worse.'

'Well that's another one we have lost, let's move on to the next.'

'Everything might not be lost, you know.'

'What do you mean, we are dead and buried.'

'Yeah I know, I was just turning something over in my mind, it's nothing, let's go and get a drink.' And the two policemen walked out of the court towards the nearest pub.

Chapter Thirty Three

Dermott was hounded by the press and was tempted to take the great sums of money offered by them for his story. But he used his calculating brain to turn the situation to his advantage. He would sell his story to as many bidders as were possible but in return he wanted publicity of the highest order. And his clever plot ensured he got it. A television interview followed, which in many people's eyes portrayed him as a shinning beacon of humanity. He offered his story to all and sundry with the proviso that all-financial benefit he received was to be passed to the national charitable AIDS foundation. The tabloids and, indeed, some of the broadsheets ran many stories, all proclaiming that this proved he was a kind and caring person and incapable of the terrible acts of which he was once accused. It worked like a dream and once more, he was back on his pedestal as the 'Expert of AIDS'. His relationship with Teresa had broken down. The unbelievable strain had been untenable for her.

Her first thought was for Simon and she insisted Dermott attend the hospital for the outstanding tests. His God had not let him down and once more, he was free to roam the universe. He was renewed with vigour and he viewed his power as his own personal fortune. He was sure he was infallible. In his darkest hours and in the depths of despair, his God always found a way for him to escape. It was all to do with his number of that he was sure. There had to be more to this than pure chance. It was fate, or providence or whatever other term he cared to use. Occasionally, when he was feeling low, he would refer to his numerology reading for solace. He found that this gave him renewed mental strength and at this precise moment in time, he needed it because he had two outstanding matters to deal with and they were both connected. Firstly, he had to travel to Ireland, to the hospital for the tests and secondly, explain to Teresa, just how closely they were related. The first task was the one that would cause him the most anguish. The fear of being found out and the consequences that would most certainly follow were a constant threat to his iron constitution.

The doctor was in his private room and on perceiving Dermott, made a gesture of surprise, which seemed to indicate that it was not the first time he had been in his presence. But he didn't comment on this and merely exchanged pleasantries instead. Just visiting the hospital was an ordeal for Dermott because his recent court case had rendered him instantly recognisable in many quarters. But he told himself that he had an automatic right to confidentiality and that both the hospital and the doctors would uphold this. Anyhow, for all the outside world knew, he could be at the hospital to offer advice on the AIDS virus.

The doctor extracted the hypodermic syringe from its neat case. With his long, white, nervous fingers, he adjusted the delicate needle and asked Demott to roll back his left shirtsleeve. His eyes rested thoughtfully on the sinewy forearm. Finally, he thrust the point home, pressed down the tiny piston and extracted the specimen he needed. 'Now,' he said glancing at Dermott with a look of curiosity. 'Should have the results of our tests in about four days, then we will have a clearer picture of how to progress this further.'

Dermott thanked him and closed the door with trepidation and tried not to look conspicuous as he walked down the corridor and out into the car park. Now he would have to wait. Mentally he was at low ebb and he would try not to think about the outcome, for the fear of the doctors uncovering his secret was a burden he could hardly bear.

His notoriety had thrust him into the public arena and he was rebuilding his reputation, he couldn't afford for a blot in his copy book at this stage of the game. After the forth day had expired, he was summoned back to the hospital and he knew this was make or break for him. He shuddered at the thought of his secret being discovered. Science and medicine had come on leaps and bounds in the last decade and he worried that 20th century knowledge would uncover his failings.

The doctor looked at Dermott over his gold-rimmed spectacles and his manner was solemn. Dermott expected the worse and for once had not prepared a suitable answer if the news were bleak.

'Well now, Dermott, I am afraid I don't have a lot of information to partake to you. Despite the progress of modern science we are not quite sure how to unravel this mystery. Are you sure you and Teresa are not related in any way?' Now Dermott was reeling. He wasn't sure how to answer. If he answered yes, he felt he might incriminate himself further. If he answered no, he might have to face the wrath of Teresa. He had a split second to make up his mind. In an instant the words were out.

'Fate has decided our poor child has to suffer in this manner and it is a cross we have to bear,' and he used a tone so full of feeling that the doctor was totally convinced Dermott had uttered the truth.

'Well, Simon has thalassaemia and because you and Teresa have the same type of genes, this is one of the causes for Simon having the genetic defects.'

'There is no treatment then?'

'I am afraid not. All we can do is try to keep your son stable, which is rather difficult with this form of defect. We shall need to see you and Teresa on a regular basis, perhaps every two months. Will that be ok?'

'Yes sure, that is fine.' And Dermott left the room feeling ecstatic. As soon as he was some distance away from the building, he punched the air with glee. He felt this had been a truly miraculous escape from justice.

He burst into his professional activities with renewed vigour, delivering speeches and talks on how to fight the AIDS virus. His reputation was very slowly but surely being rebuilt. Three weeks after visiting the hospital, he found himself giving yet another lecture in Dublin, to a very large gathering of medical aficionado. People were milling around the tightly packed room with Dermott recognising or half recognising some of his audience. At the end of his lecture, his audience were in raptures and some of them were attempting to seek Dermott's attention for a private word. His American and Canadian contemporaries collared him and he recognised other faces waiting in the background. The placid faced man, with large eyes, like saucers, looked vaguely familiar, and Dermott tried in vain to remember where he had seen him before. But he was standing too far away for Dermott to make out the discerning features. Dermott was engaged for some considerable while, as several folk came and went. Soon it became evident that the man in the background was starting to grow impatient as he shuffled up and down on the spot, glancing around nervously, as if he were keeping watch, over those entering and leaving the room. Dermott noticed his nervousness but couldn't fathom why he was eyeing up the visitors to the hall. Where had he seen this guy before? Was he a consultant? Was he a doctor? Still he couldn't remember. At length, the noise in the room began to die down as the attendees slowly dispersed. Now there was only a half dozen people left and two of them were still talking with Dermott. The stranger was still in the background, looking as if he were waiting for Dermott to finish. Dermott, was beginning to pick up the nervous vibes the man was radiating and this was now making Dermott nervous, also. Eventually, after what seemed like an eternity, the two people he had been talking to moved off, leaving Dermott free to greet the stranger. He smiled, extending a handshake, hoping that this would induce the stranger to introduce himself, and thus and sparing *him* the embarrassment for forgetting his name. But the man did not speak and Dermott was left to commence the conversation.

'Good evening, Dermott Murray, haven't we met before?' The man did not proffer a handshake.

'Yes, I am afraid we have, Mr Murray. My name is Peter White. Sergeant White, I am sure you remember me now.' Immediately it all came flooding back.

'Er, yes, you came to see me before the case. What can I do for you this time?'

'Mr Murray, would you mind coming down to the station again? I have two other colleagues waiting outside in the car.' Dermott became angry.

Not another interrogation. This was becoming too much. He had been on trial and found not guilty. What now?

'But my case is over, I have nothing more to tell you. You know I have been cleared.'

'I am sorry, Mr Murray, but this matter is not related to your case. It concerns another matter.'

'Yes, but what matter?'

'It would save a lot of embarrassment if you came down to the station sir. We just want to ask you a few questions. It shouldn't take long.'

'Well, I hope not because I have had enough of this and I am short of time. I have a flight to catch early in the morning. Judging by previous experience, these matters take forever.' Inside the car was the Inspector who had formally charged Dermott, in connection with the Patrick Mahoney case. Dermott was shaking. He didn't like this one iota. 30 minutes later, Dermott was seated in the same position, in the same chair, being questioned by the same two detectives. This was a de-ja-vu of the worst kind. Gregson began.

'Now sir, let us begin. You are Demott Murray of 3 Primrose Cottages, Kilidare and you sometimes reside on the mainland.'

'You know that is correct. What is the problem this time?'

'Please be patient, Mr Murray?'

The detective continued. 'Mr Murray, would you tell us your date of birth?'

Dermott could feel his heart start to race. He hadn't expected this question.

'6th June, 1966'

'Where were you born, Mr Murray?'

'Liverpool,' replied Dermott sharply.

'Do you have any other family, Mr Murray?' The blood drained from Dermott's face. He felt his left foot knocking under the table and his hands began to tremble. He tried his best to hide these signs by shuffling around in his seat.

'I have my mother and three sisters. They are on the mainland.' There was a pause and no one spoke for a few seconds.

'Are your sisters older than you, Mr Murray?' Dermott was losing touch with reality. It was as though someone else, a third party was answering the questions.

'Yes, I am the only boy in the family and the youngest.'

'Are you sure, Mr Murray?' Dermott was crestfallen and almost defeated.

'I have told you, I have three other sisters and there is my mother and myself. Look where is this leading to?'

'As far as you know then you have no other relations?'

'Well I have aunts and uncles and cousins.'

'Where do these cousins aunts and uncles live?' This was the question that broke the camel's back. Dermott had felt the knife, go in and now it was being pushed up to the hilt.

'All over the place.' The young detective broke in.

'Do any of them live over here, Mr Murray?' He struggled to find an answer.

'There are one or two cousins dotted about.'

'Where exactly are they dotted, Mr Murray?'

'Here and there.'

'Here and there you say.' There was a long pause before anyone spoke and the detective delivered the words as slowly as he could in order to increase the effect.

'Mr Murray, would one of these cousins happen to be Teresa Corr?'

Dermott was strangled with emotion.

'No, she is my girlfriend.'

'Your girlfriend, you say. Are you sure she is not closer than that?' Dermott's anger was rising not because of the questions, but because he had been found out.

'I don't know what you are suggesting, I have told you she is my girlfriend.'

'Can you prove that sir?'

'What do you mean, prove that?'

'Mr Murray, I think you know full well what we are suggesting. Isn't Teresa Corr related to you?'

Dermott was defeated. A stony silence followed. He did not know what to say next for fear of incriminating himself. At length he continued.

'Well, she is my cousin.'

'Your cousin, you say? Is it normal to live with your cousin?' Dermott's anger was at boiling point.

'There is no law against it is there?'

'Depends.'

'Depends on what?'

'Depends on how close you are.'

'We are close, I will grant you that.'

'Mr Murray, is there anything you wish to tell us?'

'No, nothing I can think of.'

'Well, let us tell you a thing or two. We have reason to believe you have been committing an offence, a serious offence.' Dermott braced himself for the verbal attack he knew was about to ensue.

'What offence is that?'

'We have reason to believe you have been living with your sister.' Dumfounded and stupefied Dermott was on the verge of collapse. His temples were throbbing and his heart was pounding and his concentration had gone. He had been rumbled his secret had been discovered. Now he must face the terrible consequences to follow. Weakly, he tried to defend himself. 'She is not my sister, she is my cousin.'

'Can you prove that, Mr Murray?'

'Yes, well no.'

'Come on now sir, you know the game is up. We have done some research and we have evidence that Teresa Corr is in actual fact your sister. Now what do you have to say to that?' Beaten men become optimistic men and hope then becomes an ally. He was now swimming against the tide and any branch that would get him back to the river bank he would cling to.

'Yes, we are related but she is my cousin. I couldn't have lived with my sister now, could I?' The inspector piped in. 'Now we are getting somewhere. Did you take any steps to check out she was your cousin?' Dermott coloured up, as his thoughts went back to the evening he had discovered the birth certificate.

'Well no, I have always known her as my cousin. What more should I have done?'

'Mr Murray, is there just the two of you?' No there was no going back.

'Well, I sort of adopted Teresa's son, Simon.'

'So she has a son? Who exactly does Simon belong to?'

'Simon is the son of Teresa and Eammon. Teresa and Eammon were going to be married but he passed away. He had leukaemia.' The two detectives who had been trying to build a concrete case against Dermott, now sensed that this was far more meaty and continued their questioning with renewed vigour.

'Mr Murray, are you sure Simon is not your son?'

Dermott gasped inwardly with horror. One secret had been discovered, surely they hadn't discovered his other secret?

'I have told you, I sort of adopted him.'

'Legally adopted him?'

'No, he is not adopted and he not my son. Tests can prove that.'

'Tests, what tests?' Dermott knew he had overshot the mark.

'Look, he is not my son. Teresa and I just live together.' The senior detective spoke.

'Does Teresa know you are related, Mr Murray?'

'Yes, she knows we are second cousins.'

'Would she be prepared to tell us that if we interviewed her?'

'Of course she would.'

The detective's look became grave.

'Mr Murray, I have to inform you that we have a warrant for your arrest on a charge of incest.' He continued in the usual manner.

'You do not have to say anything, but anything you do say may be given in evidence at a later date. Do you understand the charge?'

Dermott collapsed and had to be helped to his feet by the two policemen. He had gone too far this time and his God had apparently deserted him and once again he was taken into custody.

Chapter Thirty Four

A thin vale of drizzle and a thick mist engulfed the gloomy building that Dermott found himself in when he awoke the next morning. Was he awake, or was he in a dream? He found himself in the same position as when he retired, as if fixed there, his eyes swollen with weeping. The sound of someone opening the door made him start. The stranger advanced. 'Have you not slept?'

Dermott suddenly realised he was being addressed. 'I can't be sure, I feel awful.'

'Well look lively, don't you remember you have two visitors today. You asked for your advocate and ...Teresa.

The full reality began to sink in at last.He did not want to face Teresa, but the inevitable was about to happen. What was he going to say? The clock began slowly ticking down. Ten minutes, seven minutes, three minutes. God, how he wished this was over. He moved slowly to the waiting room where he was to meet with Teresa. Head bowed, legs feeling like lead, he knew the meeting was going to be unpleasant. Teresa and Peter Lever, the advocate, entered the room. Teresa's once soft complexion now looked withered and her forehead appeared etched with deep furrows. Her stern and immovable features gazed upon Dermott with a look of disdain, indescribable anger and severe incredulity. Before Dermott could speak, she launched into him with a tirade of abuse.

'You seething little scum bag. What have you done to us? Peter, here, tells me we are related.' Dermott was defeated and lost for words. The advocate realised he would have to take charge.

'Now let us keep calm and talk about this in a reasonable manner.' Teresa's abuse continued.

'You have injured me, caused a sick child to enter the world and brought misery to many, many people. I'll bet you killed Patrick Mahoney too! Even I am under suspicion, through living with you.'

'There must be a mistake, Teresa.'

'Mistake, there is no mistake. Peter has evidence here to say that Shelagh is *our* mother. How do you explain that?'

Dermott was unsure whether to lie or admit the truth. He lied.

'I don't know anything, other than we are second cousins.'

'How can we be if the hospital were asking all those strange questions. Why don't you come clean, you knew more about this than you let on.'

'No, I didn't.'

Peter Lever interjected and this time really took charge.

'Dermott, you know the charges. You are accused of living with your sister and this is a most serious charge. If it can be proved also that you have fathered Simon, then you really are in serious trouble. Let's look at the facts. The authorities say they have documentary evidence that you and Teresa are brother and sister.'

'We were not to know that!'

'Dermott in the sight of the law that is no excuse. You are *both* in deep water. Teresa has also told me about the hospital tests regarding the paternity of Simon. This is certain to come to light. It will only be a matter of time before Teresa will face charges.' Teresa spoke up. 'But if we didn't know, why should we be in trouble?'

'Teresa, the law allows for no excuses in these matters.'

'It is not Teresa's fault, I will take the blame. I will say I know about us, but that Teresa did not.'

She looked sternly at Dermott. 'Did you know?' His tone of voice was unconvincing. 'No, I didn't.' Lever continued. 'You both realise that Josie and Shelagh will be involved and the whole case will become very nasty when the press take charge. Teresa, the authorities are preparing their case against you also, so you had better be prepared. I have also been informed that you will be shortly asked to attend the hospital for further blood tests, in connection with their case preparation. These tests will carried out under supervision of the authorities.'

'But we have had these tests before.'

'Yes, but not under supervision of the authorities. You will be notified shortly.' And with that, the solemn party broke up once more and Dermott was left alone again, to ponder his future.

It was a dark hour, indeed five days later, when Dermott met Teresa at the hospital for the tests. They hardly spoke two words; such was the feelings of bitterness and sorrow between them. The allotted time span of eight hours was more than sufficient for the completion of the tests. When they were completed, Dermott asked one of his minders if he and Teresa could be allowed a little 'time to themselves' albeit under the supervision of their guardianship. He winked at one of them and asked, 'Will it be all right to visit Teresa's house for a short while?' The first detective looked at the second. 'Ok, just for a while mind you.'

'Thank you.' Teresa looked at Dermott with some suspicion. 'What do you need to come around for, there is not a lot to say?'

'No, but it will be my last hour of freedom until this is all over. Thought we could have a chat about the future.'

'Future what future? It doesn't look as if we will have a future after this.' And the conversation tapered off.

The car pulled up outside the large house whose paintwork was fading through long exposure to wind and weather. The two detectives gazed at Dermott and Teresa with watchful eyes as they entered the house.

Several minutes later the 'carer' who had been looking after Simon left for the day and once more, the family of three were left to their own devices.

'Is there anything you want me to do while I am here?' asked Dermott. 'Not really,' replied Teresa, then she paused. 'Well perhaps you could burn the old leaves and the other garden debris. It has been there for ages.'

Outside in the large garden he examined the pile of rotting vegetation. It was damp. Piling up old branches and other garden rubbish he made a large bonfire and saturated the contents with a dose of petrol. Suddenly, there was a call from inside the house. It was Teresa. 'I have made the coffee,' and with that he laid down the petrol canister and wandered back into the house. Talking and drinking coffee half an hour quickly passed. He looked at Teresa trying to gauge her reaction to him. 'No, Dermott we are not going to. I can tell by your eyes what you are up to.'

'It will be a long time after today.'

'I have told you no, there is too much hurt between us.' He pulled her towards him. 'No Dermott.' She remained cold, frigid. The pain of the recent months saw to that. Dermott was persistent and tried a softer approach. 'Just this once.'

'No, it's not right.' She wasn't going to give way this time. Pushing her on the couch he almost threw himself on top of her. She could now feel his physical contact and resisted marginally. He was aroused but his attempts at foreplay were perfunctory. Tight in a lustful embrace, he was hoping Teresa would yield, but she steadfastly refused to submit to his demands and his seed was wasted without satisfaction.

'It is no good Dermott, you have caused so much pain and anguish. It is time for you to go. Those policemen are growing agitated.' He tried to calm his ruffled appearance and looked at himself in the long bathroom mirror, adjusting his clothes at the same time. Teresa was angry again. Angry with her lover, angry with Simon, angry with herself, angry with the world in general. Pouring the coffee down the sink she stormed into the garden. She gazed upon the pile of rubbish stacked high.

'Can't even be bothered to burn the rubbish,' she said scornfully as she picked up the box of matches. The first one wouldn't light so she bent down closer to the assembled debris. She struck another and tossed it into the heart of the mound. Immediately, there was a terrible scream, and a prolonged yell of horror and anguish burst out of the silence. The frightful cry turned Dermott's blood to ice in his veins. She had been enveloped in a huge flaming ball of fire caused by the combustion of the petrol and the swirling wind and in an instant, the excruciating pain caused the spirit to cease all contact with the human form. Teresa Corr was no more. Her agonising cries had swept through the house and Dermott, that man of iron, was shaken to his soul. As he ran towards the mass of flames the vague outline hardened into a definite shape. He reached for the means to dampen the flames but it was too late, far too late. By the time he had extinguished the inferno nothing remained but a prostrate shape, the remains of the head doubled under him at a horrible angle, the shoulders rounded and the torso huddled together as if in the act of throwing a somersault. So grotesque was the attitude that Dermott could not for an instant realise, the screams had been the passing of her soul. With feverish haste, the two minders pounced on Dermott and in an instant he was rendered unconscious from the severe blow to his temple. Blood trickled from a nasty gash to his forearm and his body was bundled into the waiting vehicle.

Chapter Thirty Five

He awoke in a ward and stared up at someone in a white uniform. At first he couldn't get his eyes to focus. Was it a man or a woman he could see? Then he heard a woman's voice. 'He is coming round, better call the doctor.'

'Where am I?' Dermott muttered.

'You are in hospital. You have had a nasty blow to your head but you should be alright. The doctor will be here in a few minutes. Dermott looked up and as he was trying to build a clear picture of what had happened, he once again saw two surly minders sat at the end of the room. Slowly, it all came flooding back. The fireball, then Teresa, then a black void. A sickly feeling pervaded his whole being. After what seemed like an eternity, the medics carried out a few tests asked a few questions and left him to the mercy of the policemen. Dermott prepared himself for a verbal bashing.

'Right now, Mr Murray, let's get straight to the point. Do you remember the events of the last 12 hours?'

'Vaguely, yes.'

'Vaguely, well tell us what you remember.'

'I recall a short time at Teresa's,' his voice tapered off as tears chased one after another down his cheeks.

'You recall the fire then?'

'Yes,' he answered strangled with emotion.

'Tell us your version of events.'

'Teresa went into the garden and must have lit the fire.'

'You didn't light it then?'

'No, I was in the other room.'

'So what you are saying then is that Ms Corr set light to the fire herself.'

'Well I didn't.'

'Is it normal for a young woman in a highly emotional state to think about lighting a fire?'

'What are you getting at?'

'Mr Murray, did you not approach her with a view to having sex, the fact being she refused and you, in your pent up anger, you tried to murder her, by setting alight to the fire?' Now he knew he was in serious trouble.

'That is not true, I was in the room when the fire ignited.'

'Let's talk about the first matter. You tried to have sex with her and she refused.'

'No, that is not true.'

'Well if that is your final say on the matter, it is my duty to inform you, that we will be bringing charges against you, of the murder of Ms Teresa Corr. Have you anything further to say at this stage?'

'No, quite definitely no. I loved Teresa, I would not harm her in any way,' and with that he collapsed in a bout of uncontrollable sobbing.

Chapter Thirty Six

Dermott's urgent request to meet with both Josie and Shelagh was met with instant response. He had explaining to do indeed, but he also needed some explanation to unravel this mystery, the cause of which had now resulted in a horrific tragedy. But he immediately realised all was not well, because as they entered the visiting room, two other persons accompanied them. Yet another detective and advocate, and both were representing the prosecution. Shelagh and Josie looked at Dermott with a look of horror and disdain as if he were an evil repulsive being. Dermott spoke first. 'Who are these two, I only requested two visitors?'

The detective spoke up. 'Mr Murray, I have to inform you that we are here at the request of the prosecution. We also have written authority from the courts to attend this meeting so please hear us out. We have to inform you that you may not discuss anything that might have an influence on your forthcoming trial. As these two ladies will be called as witnesses for the prosecution, discussion of any information that may have a material influence on the trial is out of the question.' This blow was a stunner. 'This is my mother and my aunt for Christ's sake. Now you are preventing me from having a normal conversation. You want it all ways.'

Shelagh spoke next.

'In God's name Dermott, what has been going on?'

'I didn't harm her, believe me, I loved her and I didn't know she was my sister.' Shelagh and Josie both realised that *they* were under the microscope as well. It would be nigh on impossible for this conversation to continue without anyone of the three of them implicating themselves in some manner. 'You do believe me, don't you?' Josie looked at Shelagh and there was another stony silence. 'Listen, I loved her. They are saying I wilfully lived with my sister. Can't you explain? She couldn't have been my sister could she?' The advocate interrupted. 'I am sorry but the ladies are not allowed to answer that question unless in a court of law. It may have a material effect on the case.'

'What a load of rubbish,' Dermott replied angrily. 'I am sorry but you must restrict your conversation to other matters.'

'This is impossible; we are not being allowed to talk. You had both better leave mum.' With ashen faces, Josie and Dermott's mother rose to leave and Shelagh managed a few words.

'We both know you loved her Dermott, everything will work out, just wait and see,' and the meeting was instantly terminated.

Dermott felt it would be impossible for him to withstand all the pain and mental anguish that would accompany the new trial. He was now making history, but all of the wrong kind. Once again, the press had labelled him as the mixed angel. On the one hand, he was helping to fight on behalf of mankind, the terrible scourge of AIDS. His reputation was that of the angel Gabriel. On the other hand, he was classed as the fallen angel Beelzebub for his suspected crimes, all of which so far he had eluded punishment. But now he appeared to have gone that one move too far. He was notorious and was going down in history as the man who was a mixture of evil and good, and the press and public wanted a story, a good story. And most good stories end with the wicked being found guilty and then punished into eternity. That was the way that the human psyche worked. Humans by nature enjoyed watching their own suffer being dragged into the depths of despair. Did the public pity him?

No, not at all. All the species in the animal kingdom would try to help one of their own. But the human species took great pleasure in watching the slow persecution of one of their number, as long it was not they themselves involved. He was in the mire and every splash he made dragged him more slowly down into the swamp. He now faced not one but two grave charges.

The authorities regarded Dermot with bitter contempt. He had so far, somehow managed to make a mockery of their judicial system. This time they wanted him 'nailed' not just on one, but on both charges.

Enlisting the aid of George Watson, a man who had lost only three cases in his entire career, was decreed as a major coup. He was a large man with rounded shoulders a massive head and a broad intelligent face sloping down to a pointed beard of grizzled black. In court, he was a Goliath, intimidating and a man not to be messed with. He had an extensive vocabulary and he knew how to use it to good effect. Twisting the stories of witnesses and making them look foolish was second nature to him. The case of Dermott Murray was becoming as notorious as that of Dr Crippen. The presiding judge opened the case by asking how he pleaded.

'Mr Murray, you are accused of knowingly living with your sister, the late Teresa Murray, and of having full carnal knowledge of that person, so much so that as a result of your incestuous relationship, you fathered a son Simon, who unfortunately, suffers from severe physical and mental deficiencies. These deficiencies are a direct result of your incestuous affair. How do you plead?'

The jury looked on in horror as this charge was read out.

'Not guilty.'

'On a second count, you are accused of the murder of Teresa Murray on the grounds that she declined your sexual advances on the afternoon of September 12th. How do you plead?'

'Not guilty.' Dermott was to be examined firstly by his own counsel and up stepped Peter Mitchell, a man with a bold reputation but as yet untried in high profile cases.

'Mr Murray, please tell us your age.'

'I am aged 26 years.'

'How long had you known Teresa Murray or Teresa Corr as you knew her?'

'I had known her since we were children.'

'Can you be more precise about the length of time you knew her?'

'I had known her since I was four or five years old.'

'Mr Murray, what is your date of birth?'

He paused before answering.

'My date of birth is 6th June, 1966.'

'Tell me, did you know the date of birth of the late Teresa Corr?'

'Teresa was born on 30th August, 1968.'

'So, in reality you were a little over two years older than her.'

'That is correct.'

'Now would you tell us about your relationship with Teresa Murray or Teresa Corr as you knew her?'

'Teresa was my girlfriend and we had lived together for the last year or so. She was also my second cousin. There is no law against that.'

The judge intervened. 'Mr Murray, just answer the questions that are put to you. Nothing more, nothing less.'

'How long exactly had you been living together?'

'About one year.'

'Could you be more precise?'

'It is difficult to know, probably nearer nine months than a year.'

'I see, but when you embarked on this relationship, were you aware that Teresa was your cousin?'

'That is correct, she was my second cousin.'

'Did you at any time suspect she could have been your sister?'

'No never, I had no reason to and of course we would have not been able to live together.'

'Quite. Mr Murray, would you recount the events of 12th September to us. What you did throughout that day. You were, I understand, being held in Dalmunzie prison in connection with the charge his honour has just referred to.'

'That is correct. That day, however, Teresa and I had to attend the hospital to undertake tests and then late in the afternoon, I was given permission to visit her home for a short while. All under supervision of course.'

'You were left alone in the house with the deceased?'

'Yes, I was.' Several gasps of horror came from members of the jury.

'How long exactly were you alone?'

'About half an hour.'

'The two policemen supervising you remained outside, I am informed.'

'That is correct, in their car.'

'Now, would you tell us what happened leading up to the terrible tragedy?'

'Teresa asked me to burn some garden rubbish. I piled it all up and doused it with petrol. Then I left it and went back into the house.'

'Why did you leave it, Mr Murray?'

'Teresa called me. She had made some coffee and I returned inside.'

'Please continue.'

'We drank the coffee and eventually Teresa went into the garden without me knowing and lit the fire. The next thing, I heard her terrible screams and went to investigate. As you know the whole thing had exploded into a terrible fireball.'

'And by then it was too late to save her?'

'I am afraid so.'

'I know how difficult this is for you but I have to ask you. Did you at any time attempt to sexually force yourself upon her?'

'No, I did not.'

'And this dreadful incident then, are you saying was an awful accident?'

'Yes, absolutely.'

'Thank you, Mr Murray. Your honour, I wish to call Sergeant Pearson.'

'Granted.'

'Mr Pearson, on the afternoon of 12th September, you were one of the two persons who accompanied Mr Murray and Ms Corr to the hospital?'

'Yes, I was.'

'After the visit to the hospital, you allowed the accused to visit the home of Ms Corr?'

'We did.'

'Mr Pearson, is that normal procedure?'

'Well, I suppose not, but neither is it abnormal. We felt it was alright, as the accused would be unlikely to see freedom again due to the severity of the charge.'

'Please inform the members of the jury what happened that afternoon.'

'We allowed the accused to spend about half an hour with the deceased and as we were becoming anxious, we entered the house at the time of the screams of Ms Corr. We saw the accused next to the fire and it was then we realised what had happened and we pounced upon him.'

'What was he doing next to the fire?'

'It looked to us as if he had tried to throw the deceased into the fire.'

'You use the term *looked*. What do you mean?'

'Well, from the angle of her body and the posture of the accused.'

'But you cannot be certain?'

'We are certain in our mind that the accused murdered his girlfriend. He was standing next to her body as if he had pushed her into the fire.'

'Could he have been trying to remove her body from the fire?'

'I speak for both of us as witnesses and we are sure he pushed her into the fire.'

'That is all for now, Mr Pearson. You honour, I call Rory Boyd to the stand.'

Chapter Thirty Seven

'Mr Boyd, please tell us your profession and connection with this terrible case.'

'I am a senior fire officer with the fire brigade and have been so for the last 12 years. My job is to investigate suspicious or out of the ordinary cases of fire. Generally speaking, I have to decide whether causes are deliberate or accidental.'

'So, you will know not only the cause of a particular fire but also whether someone starting a fire, was trying to burn evidence of some sort?'

'In most cases, yes.'

'Does your knowledge extend to the remains of a fire, whether that be dealing with human remains or indeed other findings?'

'Yes, it does.'

'So, you could be described as a forensic fireman?'

'That is about the size of it.'

'So, Mr Boyd, what in your opinion was the cause of this tragedy?' A deadly silence prevailed over the courtroom.

'There is no doubt that the fire was caused by combustion of petrol fuel. The conditions present would allow and contribute to an explosion of this nature. The strike of a simple match would be sufficient to cause a huge fireball.'

'From your experience then, would you say that this fire was started by Teresa Corr?'

'Difficult to say for sure. There was no obvious sign of a struggle, so it could well be that Ms Corr was the victim of a pure accident. On the other hand, from the angle of the torso and the severity of the burns, she may have been pushed into the fire.'

'So, Mr Boyd, the only certainty is that the fire was started by the deceased or by Mr Murray and that fact we already know. Really we are no further forwards.'

'I am sorry I cannot be of greater assistance.'

'Thank you, Mr Boyd, no further questions.'

Now it was time for George Watson to examine Dermott and not only his appearance but also his demeanour looked particularly nasty. His body language indicated that he was about to devour Dermott in a most unsavoury fashion.

'Mr Murray, we have heard that you deny both charges brought against you but I will attempt to prove to the jury that you have been lying in a most calculating manner. You tell us that you had no knowledge that the deceased was in fact your sister. You have told us all that you always knew her as your cousin. Do you still stick to that story?'

'It is not a story, it is true.'

'Mr Murray, do you pride yourself on having a good memory?' Dermott didn't like this question for he knew not what it meant.

'Yes, I do.'

'Good.'

'Do you ever recall visiting the General Records office in Dublin?' He would have to muster all his efforts into trying to look impassive. He tried not to look in the direction of Shelagh and Josie.

'Can't say that I do.'

'Well, that is strange as I have in my possession here a photocopy of your bank statement dated May 1990. On it is a record of a cheque encashment that you wrote out to the GRO in Dublin. I have checked with the GRO and they inform me that it was probably for a copy of a birth, death or marriage certificate. Unfortunately, their records do not show names and addresses of applicants. Now I ask you did you pay for a copy of a certificate?'

Dermott shook with fear and he gripped the dock tightly.

'I do not recall paying for any document from the GRO.'

'How very convenient. Are you sure it was not a birth certificate for Teresa Murray, your sister, also known as Teresa Corr?'

'No, most definitely, it was not.'

'Well, we shall see in due course. Mr Murray, just one more question. Are you the father of the deceased's child?'

'No, I am not. The father was Teresa's previous partner.'

'Your honour, I wish to call Dr Brennan.'

'Dr Brennan, you are a specialist in treating genetic disorders and on two separate occasions you have been requested to carry out tests in connection with the accused and the late Teresa Corr?'

'Yes I have. The first time was at the request of my colleagues for a second opinion. More recently, however, I was requested for a second time in connection with this case.'

'Please, tell us what your findings were.'

'Teresa Corr's offspring suffers from a genetic disorder named thalassaemia and another genetic defect related to autism. These defects are normally borne by children whose parents are closely related for example brother and sister.' A sound of disturbance emitted from the gallery.

'Quiet in court.'

'Dr Brennan, can you say from your tests whether the accused and the deceased were brother and sister?'

'Not with certainty. Modern science has not progressed that far. However, the blood groups of Mr Murray and the deceased and that of the offspring would suggest it very likely. Certainly, the parents of Ms Corr's offspring are most likely to be closely related.'

'As closely as say brother and sister?'

'Almost pretty certainly. The odds are about ten million to one in favour of that.'

'Thank you Dr Brennan.'

The session was adjourned for a short while and allowed everyone an opportunity to gather their thoughts. When proceedings continued, Watson called another of his prime witnesses, forensic scientist, Stanley Hopkins. Watson began in high spirits.

'Mr Hopkins you are a very experienced forensic scientist with over 25 years in the profession and on 12th September you were called to the scene of the tragedy to investigate. Please, tell us what you found.'

'I was asked by the prosecution to establish if there was any evidence of a violent or sexual nature at the scene of this tragedy.'

'Did you find anything?'

'I found evidence that there had been some form of sexual encounter. There were traces of semen on the deceased's clothing, the clothing that had not been destroyed by the fire. There was also traces on the couch in the living room. This is an exact match with the DNA of the accused.' Pandemonium broke loose in the courtroom and it was several minutes before order was restored. It was looking bleak for Dermott.

'Were there any signs of violence?'

'None that I could determine. But if there was any evidence, this may have been rendered as almost useless due to the ravages of the fire on the deceased's body.'

'Thank you, Mr Hopkins, I think I will leave it there. Your honour, I have one final witness. I wish to call Mrs Shelagh Murray.' The tension in the courtroom was electric, as the grilling to come for Shelagh was crucial to the case.

Shelagh was trembling before she took the stand and the sight and sound of Watson filled her with trepidation.

'Mrs Murray, you are the mother of the accused are you not?'

She began with a whisper and the judge asked her to speak up so that the jury could hear her answers.

'Yes that is correct.'

'Mrs Murray, were you aware that your son had been living in an incestuous relationship with Teresa Corr?'

Shelagh hesitated.

'Remember you are under oath and you must answer truthfully.'

'I always knew they had a soft spot for each other, ever since they were children, but I was unaware that they had formed a relationship of some seriousness. My son's profession took him away a lot and I live on the mainland and therefore, I was not really up with events. It would have been easy for him to keep it all under a bushel. I would have no way of knowing.'

'Are you a close nit family?'

'Reasonably.'

'Would your sister Josie, who I understand, resides in Dublin, not have known about this?'

'She has told me she knew nothing of this and my son has always been a secretive person anyway.' This was a mistake by Shelagh for Watson pounced on her remark.

'Secretive you say. How very interesting. Someone who likes to keep his actions and deeds away from preying eyes. Those might be the actions of someone, who was capable of committing incest, would you say members of the jury?'

'Dermott would not do that knowingly. He is a good lad and was once studying to be a priest.'

'Yes, Mrs Murray, we are well acquainted with that history, let us just concentrate on this case shall we? Mrs Murray, would you please tell the jury how many children you have.' Now Shelagh began trembling again and she could not get her words out.

'Mrs Murray, are you unwell?' She began sobbing.

'Court is adjourned!' roared the judge.

In his chambers with the prosecution counsel, Shelagh was informed in no uncertain terms that she had to answer the questions that were put to her, no matter how painful. Three hours later, Watson began his second examination.

'Mrs Murray, please tell us how many children you have. It cannot be so difficult can it, you can count I am sure.'

'Mr Watson, not so heavy, thank you.'

'I am sorry, your honour, I apologise. Now, Mrs Murray, if we could continue.'

Shelagh started slowly.

'I actually have four, three girls and a boy.' She paused and began again. 'But I had another child after Dermott, but I didn't actually keep the child.'

'So, in fact, you have five children?'

'Well, I did.' The jury looked perplexed. The courtroom went deadly quiet, so quiet that one could have heard a pin drop.

'You did, Mrs Murray, what are you saying? Do you have five children or four children?'

'I had five but now I only have four.'

'Mrs Murray, tell us the names of your children and the order that they were born.'

'My children are Mary, Rosemary, Louise, Dermott and………'

She burst into uncontrollable fits of sobbing and with a voice strangled by emotion she whispered the word Teresa. Once more pandemonium rent the roof. Eventually Watson continued.

'Are you telling us that the deceased was your child also?'

'That is correct. Teresa was also my child but Dermott was not to know.'

'That will be for the jury to decide, Mrs Murray. Please tell us what happened to Teresa in her formative years.'

'Teresa was an accident as a result of a one-night liaison with my ex-husband Desmond. He was a drunken violent man. One time, when we were trying to sort our problems out, he raped me and I became pregnant with Teresa. My sister Josie was unable to have any children of her own, so we made a pact that my daughter would be brought up by Josie effectively as her own child. In doing so, she took the name of Corr, which was the name Josie retained after her failed marriage. We agreed not to tell anyone and have not done so to this day. My sister always treated Teresa as her own child. Those are the facts.'

'So, neither of you thought it logical to inform the authorities of these facts.'

'No, it was just an agreement between two loving sisters. We did not think there would be any harm to come from this. I had been working and living in Ireland for 12 months. Mary had been looking after the family, no one would ever know back on the mainland as I registered the birth in Dublin.'

Now some members of the jury had pity in their hearts. Pity for Shelagh and Josie.

'Mrs Murray, I think we have heard all we need to know, you may return to your place.' It looked game set and match for Dermott before Watson had commenced his summary and now he made another attack on his prey.

'Members of the jury, you have heard it all. Can you, in this day and age, expect that the accused could not have known about this incestuous relationship? You have heard from the accused's own mother that he was by nature secretive. The evidence from Dr Brennan tells you that the odds are stacked very much in favour of the child being a result of an incestuous relationship. Odds of ten million to one. The accused informs us that the child was sort of adopted and that it was not his child. Really?

'And members of the jury, what was the document he purchased from GRO? We have had no satisfactory explanation for this. Finally, let us turn to the second more serious charge. I need say no more than to remind you that Mr Hopkins found evidence of a sexual encounter. What more evidence do you need, members of the jury?'

The judge wanted to commence his summing up but Dermott's counsel asked for another witness to be called.

'Your honour, I know it is late in the day, but my witness has just flown in from Africa and I request that he take the stand.'

'Granted, although it is most unusual at this late hour.'

'Your honour, we wish to call Ralph Regal,'

Regal was a man of broad stature and a round lined and wrinkled face as if he had been exposed to extraordinary amounts of strong sunlight.

'Mr Regal, you specialise in the study of bonded African tribes do you not?'

'Yes, for those who do not recognise this form of study, it involves the study of rare tribes nearing extinction and their genetic make up.'

'In the course of your work, you have made a very deep and scientific study of incestuous and inter breeding relationships.'

'Yes, I have.'

'And it is my understanding that you are the world's leading expert in this field.'

'Some would say so.'

'You have seen the results of inter breeding and how it affects the offspring of such tribes.'

'That is correct.'

'How many years have you carried out this work?'

'18 years.'

'And how many cases of interbreeding have you studied?'

'36 cases.'

'Mr Regal, what is the normal outcome of close inter breeding of this nature? Are the offspring born with genetic defects?'

'Obviously, the risks are greater then normal, but I have only come across one case in all my studies.'

'So, in 35 of the cases, there was no abnormal defects?'

'Yes.'

'So, what is the main problem that causes these genetic breakdowns, so to speak?'

'Difficult to say without more study but I can only tell you what I have witnessed. As I say, out of 36 cases, only one resulted in the offspring having a genetic defect. This defect was of a physical nature.'

'In no way connected to autism?'

'No, not at all, the child was born with cancerous cells and lived only for three months. It died from cancer of the spleen.'

'Would you say that European white people who inter breed would have the same odds of developing a genetic defect?'

'The odds would be much less of a genetic defect.'

'Why would that be so?'

'It would take too long to explain it here as there are so many factors involved, but it has a lot to do with the way white people have evolved.'

'May I be so bold as to repeat myself, Mr Regal? You are saying that the odds of white Europeans being born with a genetic defect, as a result of inter breeding are much less.'

'Absolutely.'

'Thank you so much for your assistance, Mr Regal.'

Dermott was brimming with hope after the examination of Regal. He felt his counsel had earned their bread and his spirits rose accordingly. Now it was down to the judge.

His arrogance was there in his eyes, in every movement of his body. He displayed the look of a man who is certain, certain that the prisoner will be sent down for many years to come.

He flattered the jury, who swelled with pride, at being told they were intelligent beings who would reach a sound decision.

'Members of the jury, I am sure I do not need to remind you that you are here to decide whether the accused deliberately had an incestuous relationship with the deceased. You have heard the evidence and you have seen that the odds are millions to one in favour that the offspring is a child born from the union of Dermott Murray and Teresa Corr. We know that they were brother and sister, you have to decide if the accused knew this fact and chose to ignore it.

'You must ignore all press comments past and present, which have had an influence on this case and make your own decision based on reason. Ask yourselves if it was likely that the accused was aware of the situation or not.

'With regard to the second charge, we have heard from forensic experts. There was evidence of a sexual encounter. Did the accused take revenge on Ms Corr for rejecting his advances? Is the accused a violent man? What sort of a man is he? His own mother tells us he has a secretive nature. Some of the press have in the past described him as a champion of mankind. I cannot help you decide. The decision is yours.'

Chapter Thirty Eight

Dermott's mind and soul were so tormented he could no longer reason properly. He could no longer find lucidity and clearness of mind, and he was truly in a dismal state. Too many trials, too many questions and too much stress had weakened his iron constitution. Normally a cure for such ills has to come from within. But in Dermott's case the cure was dependent on the frailty of another human being. He found himself like a traveller in the dessert waiting for the mirage to disappear so that the waterhole can be found. His mind was cluttered up with so many facts, he had a problem remembering who had said what and when it had been said. He found this disturbing. He was on the point of giving up from despair so he repeated to himself. 'While there's life, there's hope.'

After eight days, the jury declared they had not reached a verdict on either charge and once more, the judge informed them he would accept majority verdicts. The usual disagreements were taking place. One juror was accusing another of being influenced by the press. It was consciences that were holding up a decision. Each one of the jurors had their own skeletons in the cupboard, no matter how small. The prosecution had swung the trial in their own favour in a masterly way. Too much evidence delivered with damming effect. How much longer had Dermott to wait? Three more long days elapsed, 72 long hours and then, the jury returned to the chamber. 'Have you reached a verdict?'

The foreman rose slowly trying to calm his manner. 'We have reached our verdict, your honour.'

'On the first case, how do you find the accused?' Silenced reigned, once more there was a slight pause.

'Not guilty, your honour.' Gasps of incredulous surprise could be heard. Someone called out.

'Well done, Dermott.'

Immediately the judge intervened. 'Remove that man from the gallery,' and then a scuffle broke out as the perpetrator was led away.

'Is that the decision of you all?'

'Yes, your honour.'

'On the second charge, that of the murder of Teresa Corr, how do you find the accused?'

Surely it could not keep happening. How many times was Beelzebub going to get off Scot-free? This was becoming a joke. Jurors were there to listen to the facts and then make a reasonable decision.

'GUILTY, your honour!' and the foreman let the words come out slowly as if to ensure that no one could miss-hear them. Dermott collapsed and his co-ordination seemed to become clumsy.

'Quiet in my court. Is that the decision of you all?'

'Yes, your honour.'

'Quiet in my court. Get the accused to his feet please.' As Dermott was helped to his feet, his head began to swim and he barely heard the words that the judge spoke.

'Accused, you have heard the verdict of the jury. I have no choice but to sentence you to imprisonment for life and I recommend that you serve a minimum of 25 years.' And with the noise in the background, Dermott stumbled into the arms of two court officials and was then led away completely mesmerised.

Chapter Thirty Nine

It was three days before he could think clearly and take in the enormity of his situation. Stress began to take effect. For some strange reason, he found his vision was now impaired. His hair was suddenly greying at the temples and he felt and looked visibly fatigued. He was listless irritable and refused to accept visitors. On the fifth day, he felt a cold coming on and requested the medic prescribe some remedy. The effects were short lived and seven days later, he felt once more that his health was deteriorating badly. The warders were secretly in awe of him but several of them were in a strange way fond of him, because even though he was an evil specimen himself, he had been fighting the evil of AIDS on behalf of his fellow man. Two months elapsed and his masterful personality still decreed no visitors but he was now indeed becoming a deplorable spectacle.

His gaunt, wasted face, staring from his bed, sent a chill to the warders' heart. A specialist was sent in to examine the patient who was now reduced to a withering specimen. Loss of memory, impaired breathing appeared to be ebbing his life away.

He needed his God quite badly.

One more month passed away, 30 long days. His eyes began to assume the brightness of fever. There was a hectic flush on either cheek and dark crusts clung to his lips: his thin hands began to twitch incessantly; his voice was croaking and spasmodic. Occasionally, because he was so weak, he seemed unable to fathom what were thoughts and what were dreams and he vaguely remembered that this had happened once before in his life. That was the time when he had read and re-read and finally digested the contents of Jung's book 'A Biography of the Devil'.

Some days, however, he felt stronger and his razor sharp mind would return and it was at moments such as these that he felt he could once more take on the world and all that it had to offer. But the symptoms would return and the face would become convulsed with the horrendous pain that racked his strained body.

He was beginning to feel that he could no longer control his bodily movements and he felt sure he knew what the prognosis would be. He did not want to face up the facts.

In one of his more lucid moments, he requested that his advocate be allowed to visit as soon as was possible. He hoped that on the day of the visit, he would be able to remember what he wished to say and he summoned all his strength and willpower on the day of the meeting. With the strength of Hercules he whispered.

'Listen, I need you to set the wheels in motion with the authorities. Get them to allow you access to Eammon Dunphy's medical records, especially for the period just before he died. It is important for other folks……. not just for me. It is too late for me……….. I have AIDS. The only possible cause of the infection is via Teresa and that implicates Dunphy and may affect other partners he had. See what you can do. I know it will take forever, if ever at all, but please do it.'

A week later the 'prince of darkness' passed away in his sleep. It was only on the 6th of June, 1999, years later, that permission was granted for access to Eammon Dunphy's medical records. Numbers had generally dictated Dermott Murray's erratic life, and just like his life, the numbers became mixed up along the way. When the medical records were finally examined, there were obviously many notes regarding the fact that Eammon Dunphy was being treated for leukaemia. In addition, there was also an addendum stating that Eammon Dunphy had contracted the AIDS virus.

John Pickersgill's first book Looking For The Real Me is a true story about his lifetime search for his origins and birth mother. Written from the heart with passion, feeling and genuine experience and understanding of what it is like to struggle against adversity, John believes that most obstacles in life can be overcome with drive, determination and great tenacity, attributes he has in abundance.

It is no surprise therefore that he is able to draw on his life experiences and builds them into his first novel, 'The Sign Of The Devil'. He cleverly lives and breathes the characters so as to bring them alive in the plot with a narrative style that is unrelentingly direct and very powerful. Detailed descriptions of the processes and places he has encountered in his own life blend with the storyline that has a sufficiently high concept to make it totally original and yet at the same time a realistic and believable plot.

John continues to play 5 a side football, walks, scrambles and climbs mountains and goes running several times a week. Originally from Manchester he lives in Bedfordshire and has nearly completed a second novel From Daughter To Mother. The inspiration therefore for The Sign of the Devil comes from within and is based on a life experience of knowing what it is like to cope with rejection and struggle against adversity.